I0761906

the deception code

(a remi laurent fbi suspense thriller—book 5)

ava strong

Ava Strong

Bestselling author Ava Strong is author of the REMI LAURENT mystery series, comprising six books (and counting); of the ILSE BECK mystery series, comprising seven books (and counting); of the STELLA FALL psychological suspense thriller series, comprising six books (and counting); and of the DAKOTA STEELE FBI suspense thriller series, comprising three books (and counting).

An avid reader and lifelong fan of the mystery and thriller genres, Ava loves to hear from you, so please feel free to visit www.avastrongauthor.com to learn more and stay in touch.

ISBN: 978-1-0943-9492-3

BOOKS BY AVA STRONG

REMI LAURENT FBI SUSPENSE THRILLER
THE DEATH CODE (Book #1)
THE MURDER CODE (Book #2)
THE MALICE CODE (Book #3)
THE VENGEANCE CODE (Book #4)
THE DECEPTION CODE (Book #5)
THE SEDUCTION CODE (Book #6)

ILSE BECK FBI SUSPENSE THRILLER
NOT LIKE US (Book #1)
NOT LIKE HE SEEMED (Book #2)
NOT LIKE YESTERDAY (Book #3)
NOT LIKE THIS (Book #4)
NOT LIKE SHE THOUGHT (Book #5)
NOT LIKE BEFORE (Book #6)
NOT LIKE NORMAL (Book #7)

STELLA FALL PSYCHOLOGICAL SUSPENSE THRILLER
HIS OTHER WIFE (Book #1)
HIS OTHER LIE (Book #2)
HIS OTHER SECRET (Book #3)
HIS OTHER MISTRESS (Book #4)
HIS OTHER LIFE (Book #5)
HIS OTHER TRUTH (Book #6)

DAKOTA STEELE FBI SUSPENSE THRILLER
WITHOUT MERCY (Book #1)
WITHOUT REMORSE (Book #2)
WITHOUT A PAST (Book #3)

PROLOGUE

A mansion overlooking the Potomac River, just south of Washington, DC.
5:30 AM

Valentina Montero hummed cheerfully to herself as she punched the security code into the keypad next to her employer's front gate. Señor Grayson was an early riser, so she had to make his coffee and eggs, turn on the heat in the breakfast room, and then get started with the morning's cleaning.

The giant ironwork gate clicked, then hummed open on its hinges. Valentina drove through, hit a button to shut the gate behind her, then drove up the long driveway past a beautifully manicured lawn, barely visible in the predawn autumn light, and up to the rambling Gothic-style mansion overlooking the river. Señor Grayson had told her it had been originally built by some railroad tycoon in the nineteenth century. To her it looked like everybody's stereotype of a haunted castle, but her boss liked old things.

As she passed the house, she noticed that the lights in a couple of the collection rooms on the ground floor were on. Señor Grayson must have gotten up early. He was too meticulous to leave lights on overnight.

Valentina drove around to the back of the house to the service entrance and parked.

As she switched off the engine and got out of the car, she chuckled to herself. Señor Grayson never tired of looking at his own collection, just like she never tired of visiting the Smithsonian. So many things to see at the Smithsonian, everything from Lindbergh's airplane to three-thousand-year-old bronzes from China.

Señor Grayson had some three-thousand-year-old Chinese bronzes too, but there was only one *Spirit of St. Louis*. If the Smithsonian didn't already own it, he would have probably bought that too. It would look nice hanging from the ceiling of the great hall in front of that grand marble staircase. It would certainly be more fun to clean than that huge chandelier that had once hung in a French mansion during the time of Louis XIV.

She let herself in, punched the code to switch off the burglar alarm, and walked down the hallway to the kitchen. Even here, where only she and the other two servants ever came, the walls were adorned with items from Señor Grayson's collection. A Folsom arrowhead from 7000 BC. A little intaglio from some Roman ring, engraved with the figure of Mercury. An engraving of the Karnak temple by David Roberts.

When Valentina had applied for this job all those years ago, Señor Grayson had been kind enough to take her on a tour of his collection and she had surprised him with the depth of her historical knowledge. She had explained that when she was a little girl in Mexico City, she had loved visiting the Museo Nacional de Antropología with its giant Aztec sun calendar and its impressive gold artifacts. She had dreamed of growing up to become an archaeologist.

But little girls from poor barrios did not grow up to become archaeologists, and she had become a maid in America instead. At least all that reading got her a job cooking and cleaning in one of the biggest private collections in the United States.

And she shouldn't complain, she thought as she flicked on the kitchen light and surveyed its large interior and gleaming appliances. She had worked hard and saved. Her husband, Fernando, a welder, had worked hard and saved. And now their three children were all in college. Her son was in his first year of law school on a full scholarship. Her daughters were studying accounting and theater.

Valentina had never understood why some people born here criticized their country so harshly. Sure, it wasn't perfect, but it had given her so much. It would give her children more.

As she put on the coffee, Yemeni coffee made in an Italian coffeemaker and served black just the way her boss liked it, she decided to go check on him. If he had risen early, he might want his breakfast right away rather than wait until after his coffee like he usually did.

She headed up a short flight of steps to the ground floor, which was slightly raised above ground level so that guests coming through the front door could first go up three steps of Italian marble past a pair of

Greek statues. As she walked along, she passed several framed early woodcuts, including three originals from Dürer, and into a hallway leading to one of the exhibition rooms.

And that's when she realized something was wrong.

This exhibition room was dedicated to numismatics, with a vast collection of Roman and Greek coins along with examples from Medieval Europe and even some very rare early Anglo-Saxon coins. They were arranged in glass-topped cabinets with shelves beneath.

Even though the light was switched off, she could see all the shelves were open. Señor Grayson never left shelves open. He was an extremely tidy man.

Valentina's first thought was that Bruce had visited. Señor Grayson's useless rich boy son. All cocaine and empty conversation and a condescending attitude toward the "help," even though every single member of staff was more intelligent and far harder working.

Had Bruce gone on one of his binges? She'd seen them before and they weren't pretty. Tripping over things or throwing them in a childlike tantrum. When he was younger, before getting his inheritance, he even stole from his father, as if he didn't have enough money!

She'd stopped buying lottery tickets because of him. She'd rather not be a millionaire if that's what it would turn her children into.

She looked down the hallway. It ran past another exhibition room and then into the front hall. Beyond its marble-floored expanse she could see another hallway with two more exhibition rooms. The lights weren't on in the wing where she stood or in the opposite hallway, but lights shone from both exhibition rooms there.

Valentina was about to turn on the hallway light and call out for Señor Grayson and Bruce, but something stopped her.

Instead, she stood and listened. She could hear something.

The sound of drawers opening, and someone muttering angrily to himself.

Bruce! She should have known. That no-good rich boy was probably looking for some cocaine he had stashed somewhere. His drug-addled mind often forgot where he hid his supply and he'd launch into furious searches that tore the place up.

One of the great satisfactions of Valentina's job was knowing that most of the time he'd never find his stash. Any time she came across some of his drugs, she'd flush them down the toilet. The look on Bruce's face was worth the extra cleaning.

His father, a successful businessman, called her Señora Montero and lent her books. The useless son called her "hey you" and never did anything with his life. Yes, she truly enjoyed those flushing sessions. She couldn't calculate how many thousands of dollars' worth of cocaine she had flushed.

Maybe she'd catch Bruce doing something bad enough that he'd get forbidden from entering the house. He could scuttle off to one of the other houses and leave the staff and his long-suffering father in peace.

Quietly she walked down the unlit hall, then out into the grand entrance. She did not glance at the ancient statues and fine paintings, or the grand staircase and its immense crystal chandelier. Normally she would stop for a moment when she passed through to admire these things. Not today. She was a woman on a mission.

More clattering and thumping. More cursing. Bruce must have really gone on a bender.

She entered the hallway on the other side of the grand entrance. The first exhibition room lay open and lit to her right. She moved to the doorway and looked inside.

And brought her hand up to her mouth as her lips formed an astonished O.

What a mess! This was the Medieval Room. Weapons. Armor. Illuminated manuscripts. Byzantine icons. Ottonian ivory carvings. All set up with museum-quality lighting and cases.

And now it looked like it had been hit by a whirlwind.

All the display case drawers were open. The icons had been taken off the walls. The armor lay in pieces scattered all over the floor.

Bruce had searched through everything, making a mess of his father's collection. At least he had the respect and good sense not to break anything. The search looked like it had been hurried and desperate, and yet done with care.

Because if that useless young man had actually broken any of his father's priceless collection, he might be cut off. Bruce had never shown any interest in the private museum he had grown up in. Nothing mattered to him except his own pleasure.

The sounds of a frantic search continued in the next exhibition room. Valentina frowned and stomped over to the doorway, no longer trying to hide her approach. She was going to have words with Bruce Grayson. Strong words. It didn't matter that he was the boss's son. His behavior was unacceptable.

"Señor—" she started, and then cut off.

Because as she made it to the doorway of the Classical Room, as messed up as the Medieval Room, she stopped short.

Señor Grayson lay face down in a pool of dried blood, his gray hair matted like a giant scab. And it was not his son who had stopped his search to whirl around and stare at her standing in the doorway.

No, it was someone else entirely.

Someone rushing at her with a bloody hammer.

"No!" was all she managed to scream before the hammer came down.

And within moments, Valentina Montero lay next to her employer, two admirers of the past—one rich, one working class—bludgeoned to death amid the collection they had both loved.

CHAPTER ONE

The Appian Way in the suburbs of Rome, that same day

Despite the danger that they had been followed, despite the need to hurry, Professor Remi Laurent could not help but slow down and look around her in wonder.

She and her partner at the FBI, Special Agent Daniel Walker, strolled down a leafy, cobblestoned avenue. On both sides of the road stretched wide fields, the bucolic view marred somewhat by a cluster of distant apartment buildings to the left. But keep your eyes forward and all you saw was an overgrown road and a couple of old stone monuments on the edge of it.

This was no ordinary road. It was one of the best preserved stretches of the Appian Way, built in 312 BC by the Roman censor Appius Claudius Caecus, expanded over the centuries, and long used by the glorious capital of the Empire as one of the main roads in and out of the city. Leading families, eager to show off their pedigree, built sumptuous tombs along its length, complete with marble plaques boasting of their ancestors' deeds.

They approached one of those tombs now, a temple in miniature, cracked Corinthian columns still holding up a portion of the roof. Inside lay a pair of shattered sarcophagi. The inscription had vanished, stolen by relic hunters in the early modern period or taken by archaeologists in the twentieth century to one of Rome's innumerable museums.

A pity either way. It would be nice if the monuments of the past could remain where they were, safe from acquisitive hands.

But that wasn't how the world worked. If her career as a medievalist hadn't taught her that, her investigations for the FBI certainly had.

"I think someone's following us," Daniel whispered, confirming a sneaking suspicion they had both had since arriving in Italy. "No. Don't look around. Too obvious. Let's go look at this tomb."

They stopped and stared at it. Daniel took out his phone and took a picture of the tomb. As he angled it so she could see he whispered, “Don’t look at the phone, look beyond it. Two men, tan slacks. Dress shirts.”

She looked where he indicated. Several people were in view. An Italian family with a picnic basket looking for somewhere to set up. An old man in dirty clothes carrying a burlap sack, perhaps one of the local farmers. An American tourist couple with a huge camera.

And then the two well-dressed men who had just stopped. One was pointing out into a field and the other looked on, grinning.

Remi and Daniel had just passed that way, and there was nothing worth pointing at, just a field with some cows. Obviously these two men had stopped in order to pretend they were doing something, just like she and Daniel had.

“Looks like the Society of Devout Students has figured out that wall painting too,” Remi grumbled.

They had first learned of the existence of that secretive society, dedicated to the protection of the Gospel of Longinus, on an earlier case. Unfortunately, the society had learned of Remi and her hunt for the cryptex, and decided to try and find it for themselves.

Only a couple of months before, they had even followed her all the way to her latest clue, a faded fresco in the ancient St. Pishoy Monastery in the desert of Wadi El Natrun, Egypt. It had taken Remi many long hours studying photos of the fresco to figure out the message hidden inside it. There had been no text other than a few names and common prayers, but the pictures had seemed unusual.

So every night, after her grueling accelerated training to make her an FBI agent, she brewed some coffee and stared at the images.

And stared.

Weeks of staring and it had finally come to her—the picture was a series of symbols, like most church paintings, but also a clue.

Or series of clues.

It showed Christ, robed and dusky like an Egyptian, reaching out his hand, two fingers extended in the old method of giving a blessing. His fingers pointed to a book, no doubt the Bible, being held by a young man. Next to this scene was a small, stylized city with the Coptic word for Rome painted above it. Beneath the city was a winged lion, the symbol for St. Mark, one of the four gospel saints and the founder of the Coptic church. Next to this figure was an altar laid out with candles and the objects for Communion.

The one detail that caught Remi's eye the most was a line between the city and St. Mark and the altar. Grass grew out of it, signifying ground. Ground was hardly ever painted in early Christian art. Figures simply floated. Its inclusion here must have held some special significance to the artist.

Once she saw that, all the pieces began to fall into place.

St. Mark under Rome. The Catacombs of St. Mark just outside of Rome. Inside these tunnels for early Christian burials was a chapel dedicated to St. Mark, from which that network of catacombs got their name.

A mural in a monastery far out in the desert of Egypt pointed here, to the early Christian catacombs along the Appian Way just outside Rome. One of the world's oldest functioning monasteries pointed to one of the world's oldest Christian burial places.

When Christianity had been a minority religion in the Roman Empire, persecuted by pagan emperors angered that the Christians wouldn't bow down to them as living gods, the Christians had dug a network of tunnels to bury their dead. Instead of triumphant monuments along the Appian Way with inscriptions dedicating the souls of the departed to Rome's many gods and goddesses, the Christians buried their dead in secret, out of sight.

The catacombs naturally became meeting grounds for the illegal faith, and besides the tombs there were chapels and meeting rooms. The St. Pishoy Monastery rebus pointed to one specifically—the so-called Catacombs of St. Mark, given its name because of the chapel and several paintings of the winged lion that was the saint's symbol.

When the answer came to her it hit her like a sledgehammer. Could the secret of the cryptex finally be in her grasp? After all the clues, was the end to her quest finally in reach?

Then came the doubt. The Catacombs of St. Mark had been rediscovered in the late eighteenth century during building works. Treasure hunters, archaeologists, and curiosity seekers had been poking around the catacombs ever since. It was the same with all the other tunnel networks built by ancient Christians. Many had suffered serious damage because of this before the Italian government started to protect them around the turn of the century.

Then there was another doubt. The mural of St. Pishoy Monastery had been painted in the ninth century, long after the conversion of the Emperor Constantine in 313 AD had made Christianity a legal religion in the Roman Empire. Soon it became the dominant religion. Within a few more generations, it was paganism that was banned. The catacombs, no longer useful, were sealed and gradually forgotten.

So by the time of the Egyptian painting and the construction of the cryptex in the Middle Ages, did anyone even know the Catacombs of St. Mark even existed?

Remi decided that they must have. Considering all the secret societies, hidden agendas, and forbidden texts secreted within the vast world of Christianity, a truth that she had only recently come to understand, anything was possible.

And so she had requested some vacation time, purportedly due to exhaustion and a case of nerves thanks to their last case, and booked a flight to Italy. Daniel, also taking some vacation time, had volunteered to come along. He had become almost as eager for the hunt as she had.

But it turned out the Society of Devout Students had cracked the code as well.

Or had they? Remi wondered as she glanced at the two burly men trying very hard to look innocuous. The society had agents everywhere, especially Italy. In fact, their headquarters was in Rome, only a few kilometers away. If they had cracked the code about the same time she had, they should have come and gone by now.

Unless they hadn't cracked the code. Unless they were monitoring her movements and had followed her here.

It had happened before, when a case had taken her to Luxor. Father De Sanctis of the society had snuck into the local museum, thinking she was having a secret meeting about the cryptex with the director.

"We need to lose them," Remi said.

"Easier said than done," Daniel replied. "We're out in the open and the catacombs are only another kilometer up the road. Our tour is in half an hour, by the way."

Remi nudged him. "You can be late. You're always late."

"I'm not always late!"

Remi smiled. "Just most of the time."

"We're both going to be late if we don't shake these guys."

Remi studied the tomb they were pretending to photograph. Behind it stood a thin hedge, blocking the view of what she assumed was a field behind it.

A chain strung between two metal poles blocked entrance to the otherwise wide-open tomb. Enough to stop the law-abiding general public, but not an FBI trainee agent on vacation. She stepped over the chain.

"Here we go," Daniel grumbled, following her.

Resisting the urge to look at the two men following her, she pointing at some imaginary item of interest within the tomb and passed between the columns, Daniel by her side.

Like she had suspected while standing outside, it felt like entering a Roman temple in miniature. There was even an altar, a rectangular stone with Latin writing on it and the bas-relief of a robed woman slumped in grief. The top was bare, with a raised circular portion for burnt offerings.

Beyond this stood the two sarcophagi, made of fine porphyry but now shattered, most likely by treasure hunters long ago. Despite the urgency of their situation, Remi paused to look, tut-tutting at the wanton destruction.

Don't judge too harshly, she reminded herself. *You're a bit of a treasure hunter yourself.*

At least you're a less destructive one. Most of the time.

She still hadn't forgiven herself for smashing that medieval ceramic figurine of the Virgin Mary. But what could she do? The clue it contained was hidden inside. It had been made to be smashed.

That was before it was an antique.

Remi put that thought aside and looked around for an escape from the men following her.

The back wall had entirely disappeared, only the bare corner columns still standing, holding up nothing. A few stones lying overgrown in the weeds were all that remained.

Luckily the side walls remained intact, shielding them from view.

"That hedge looks thin enough to push through," Remi said.

"Sure, I don't mind getting scraped up on my vacation," Daniel replied.

"I'll buy you a pizza and a gelato."

"You know my heart."

They peeked out the back of the tomb, looking both ways. The thin strip of the Appian Way they could see from their vantage point was empty. Their pursuers would be here any moment, though. Time to make a move.

Clambering over the heap of rubble, they got to the hedge and, covering their faces to protect them from the branches, pushed their way through. Remi's blouse caught and got a little tear. Her hands got scratched in several places. A small price to pay.

They stepped through and onto the edge of a broad green field. A few cows grazed placidly not far off, ignoring the two intruders.

"There," Remi whispered. A low stone fence divided this field from the neighboring one not twenty yards to their left. They made for it, trying to run quickly yet silently. Remi was glad she'd worn running shoes. She hadn't worn heels since she had joined the FBI. She wondered if she would ever wear them again.

Low voices on the other side of the hedge. The Society of Devout Students or just some tourists?

They didn't pause to find out. Hurrying to the wall, they hopped over it and crouched behind, now fully out of sight.

"What do we do now?" Daniel whispered.

Good question. She looked around. The field they were now in lay fallow. A farmhouse stood in the distance. Remi hoped the farmer didn't look out the window and see two strangers hiding behind his boundary wall. The hedge ran along the Appian Way, cutting off the tourist site from private land. It looked thin enough in many places to push back through.

Good, so they could get back to the Appian Way and continue on to the catacombs, but the two men from the society would be sure to find them.

Unless …

Remi peeked over the wall and saw a man push his head and shoulders through the hedge. He was looking the other way. Remi ducked back down before he looked her direction.

Of course. It wouldn't have taken them long to figure out she and Daniel weren't in the tomb anymore. They must have realized the only way for them to have disappeared was to have pushed through the hedge. They had probably broken enough of the little branches to leave a clear sign of their passage.

So the men would come through and start searching for them. And she and Daniel had nowhere to hide.

Just then Daniel's phone buzzed.

"Are you serious?" Remi asked, exasperated.

"Sorry. I have this filtered. It must be important."

Still crouched behind the wall, he checked his phone. Remi looked over his shoulder and saw it was an email from Keiko Ochiai, assistant director of the Antiquities Division.

"What does she want?" Remi whispered. "We're on vacation."

"Pro tip: no one gets a vacation from the FBI."

He opened the email and angled the phone so she could read it.

"Daniel, there's a case that requires your immediate attention. Can you and Remi make it back by tomorrow? Apologies, Keiko Ochiai."

Daniel started typing.

"Dear Assistant Director, we will try to book the next flight. Regards, Special Agent Daniel Walker."

Remi gasped. "What are you doing? We have work to do here."

"It wasn't a request, it was an order. The FBI doesn't really make requests. At least we get a two for one."

"A two for one?"

"If you get recalled from vacation, you get two days for every one you miss."

"That doesn't help us get into the catacombs before they do!"

"Keep your voice down," Daniel said. "This is your fault anyway. You have an incredible talent for getting us into trouble. We're halfway around the world trying to sneak into some ancient catacombs and Assistant Director Ochiai wants us to come in."

"Why does that count as getting into trouble?" Remi asked.

Daniel looked at her, cocking an eyebrow. "Have you not been paying attention on our previous four cases?"

Remi laughed, then clapped a hand over her mouth. That had been too loud.

"We'll need to change our flight. But don't worry, we still have plenty of time to get there," Daniel reassured her. "We just need to hide out for a bit and give them the slip."

"Hey, you two!" a man's gruff voice shouted in Italian. "What are you doing here? This is private property!"

CHAPTER TWO

Remi hissed in fear and frustration. Less than a kilometer away from the catacombs, and now some irate farmer was going to call the police on them. What terrible luck!

But where was the farmer?

Remi looked all around and didn't see anyone else on their side of the stone fence. Then she realized the shouting came from the other side.

"Yes, you! There's nothing to see here."

Remi peeked over the wall again. A middle-aged farmer, all strong arms and scowl, stomped across the pasture toward the two men from the Society of Devout Students, who had pushed through the hedge and stood at the edge of the field.

The two men didn't even bother to answer. They simply looked around, Remi ducking down, and then when she dared a peek again she saw them passing back through the hedge.

"Now what?" Daniel asked.

Good question. They were safe for the moment, but their pursuers knew roughly where they were. They would assume Remi and Daniel would either skirt the Appian Way in the direction they had been heading since they got off the bus a couple of kilometers up the road, double back and return the way they came, or strike off across the fields.

The sound of a car gave her an idea. On the opposite side of the fields from the Appian Way stood a scattering of trees and bushes, and as she looked she could just see the top of a car passing by on a sunken road. She watched, and the car moved along, paralleling the Appian Way before going out of sight behind the farmhouse and a row of closely planted trees.

"Let's get on that road," she said, pointing.

"Good idea," Daniel agreed. "I'll turn on Google Maps and when we get parallel to the catacombs, we can cut across the fields and get to it."

It seemed like a sound plan, but the stone wall was so low they had to crawl the whole way to the road so as not to get spotted by that irate man protecting his cows.

Daniel grumbled all the way. Remi couldn't make out most of what he said, but the words "extra-large gelato" were among them.

"You and your stomach," Remi chuckled.

"You and your historical obsessions."

"Touché."

They got to the road—a narrow, two-lane affair—and slid down a low embankment to get onto the shoulder. They walked along it. Only rarely did a car pass. Daniel got on his phone and brought up their position on Google Maps.

"We're almost there," he announced. "Isn't technology a wonderful thing?"

"They have it too," Remi said, looking around nervously. "What if they brought a car and decide to check this road?"

"Then we give them nothing. We leave and come back another day."

"Another day? We can't afford to wait another day!"

"I don't think they've figured it out. I think they're simply following us. Riding on your research's coattails. I'm sure you've had rival academics do that before."

Remi smiled ruefully. "Indeed I have."

They came to the spot indicated on the map and found themselves beside another pasture with a few grazing cows. They waited for an oncoming car to pass before hopping a low fence and making their way across.

Remi checked her watch. The tour would start in ten minutes. They had to time this just right. If they got there too soon, the men following them would have a better chance of coming across them. Too late, and they wouldn't get in. Each system of catacombs only allowed a limited number of people in per day in order to preserve the fragile monuments.

They crossed the field without seeing anyone and got to the hedge. Google Maps showed the entrance to the Catacombs of St. Mark to be right on the other side. They paused for a minute, unsure when to break through and reveal themselves before the sight of a farmer walking in the next field over prompted them to make a move.

They chose the worst possible time. Just as they pushed through a thin part of the hedge, spotting a small, nineteenth-century brick building put atop the catacomb entrance with a sign advertising it, a crowd of tourists came out the door. The previous tour. A few other people stood nearby waiting to join the tour she and Daniel had signed up for.

They all stared at the two people breaking through a hedge.

"Hi!" Daniel said in a cheerful tone. "Call of nature. Didn't want to be caught short in the catacombs, eh?"

Remi rolled her eyes.

One of the men grinned, pointed to the dirt on their knees, and said in an English accent, "Looks like you were doing more than having a slash, mate."

Several giggles from the crowd. Remi felt the urge to sink through the ground.

Most of the crowd dispersed as the previous tour moved on and the few people for the next one lined up. As she brushed off her pants, Remi took a look around. No sign of the men from the Society of Devout Students.

They passed through a narrow doorway, an attendant checking the electronic tickets on their phones, and assembled in a small foyer. A few photos of the catacombs hung from the walls. The others studied them as Remi fidgeted.

"Relax," Daniel whispered. "We shook them."

"I'll relax when we get to the Chapel of the Four Gospel Evangelists."

"Hello, everyone!" a young woman called in English from the doorway that she was locking. Apparently she was the only employee here. "Welcome to the tour. My name is Anke van der Berg. I am a Dutch graduate student at the Classics and Ancient History department at Sapienza University in Rome."

Remi nodded in appreciation. That was the best department in Italy, and courses were taught in Italian, so this woman's Italian must be as good as her English. She seemed intelligent and eager, the kind of enthusiastic graduate student that Remi appreciated.

And that made her feel very bad about the terrible, horrible thing they planned to do to her. Remi hoped it wouldn't cost this nice young woman her job.

She hoped it wouldn't cost Remi and Daniel their jobs either. At least they had paid for their tickets with an anonymous app.

"Construction of the Catacombs of St. Mark began in the second century A.D., around the same time as several of the other networks of catacombs along the Appian Way. The tunnels and tombs run for more than five kilometers on three levels. In this tour we will see just a part of them, the most stable tunnels with the best artwork."

Except for the Chapel of the Four Gospel Evangelists, Remi added silently. *That's a bit too out of the way, at the end of a supposedly unstable tunnel. Or did someone in the Italian government just say it was unstable to keep the chapel from prying eyes?*

Anke went on.

"We'll head on down those stairs right over there. While you are on the tour, please watch your head because the ceiling is low in places and please do not stray from the lighted path."

Daniel snickered. Remi elbowed him.

"So if you'll follow me, we can—oh!"

A furious pounding at the door made her open it.

"Sorry we're late," said a brusque voice. Remi's heart clenched. She recognized that voice.

A moment later her worries were confirmed as Father De Sanctis of the Society of Devout Students walked in, his two goons in tow.

She had a bit of history with this man. On an earlier case, he had been a suspect in murdering a string of members of his society, although in the end it turned out he was only hiding out, thinking he would be the next victim.

Father De Sanctis was an older man with a neatly trimmed white beard, but he was fit and healthy. Remi knew this because she had fought him once, back when she tried to detain him on suspicion of murder. She won, but only because she pepper sprayed him. He hadn't forgiven her for that, and given his overall personality she hadn't regretted it either. Was feeling good about pepper spraying a priest a sin? She wasn't sure. The nuns at her Catholic school had never covered that topic.

"Welcome to the tour, Father," Anke said in a perky voice, noticing his priest's collar. "You're just in time. We were about to head downstairs. You almost missed us."

Father De Sanctis looked right at Remi and smiled. "I wouldn't miss this for the world."

Remi and Daniel exchanged glances. Her partner gave her a brief, reassuring nod as if to say, "This changes nothing."

Darn right it doesn't. If we could have put them off the trail I wouldn't have minded coming back tomorrow. But now that they're here, now that they know the answer lies in the catacombs, we're going to have to go through with it.

That simultaneously thrilled and terrified her.

The visitors began to file down the stairs. Father De Sanctis got right behind Remi and whispered into her ear, "You're not as clever as you think you are."

"We'll see about that," she grumbled.

They walked down a narrow staircase. A cool breeze wafted up from below. Remi ducked a little from the low ceiling, hoping Father De Sanctis would bump his head. Sadly he didn't.

They ended up in a small room from which two stone tunnels branched. The tunnels were narrow enough that Remi could have spread her arms and put her palms flat on both walls. The arched ceiling was almost low enough to touch. Lights were strung at far intervals along the ceiling, giving a dim light. They were powered by a switchbox by the staircase. Daniel positioned himself next to it. She and her partner had memorized the layout of the catacombs from an archaeological report before they came, and knew exactly where they were going.

Once the visitors were all assembled, the tour guide turned to them. "Our first stop will be down this hallway, where we will see one of the oldest Christian tombs in the catacombs. You'll notice on the wall is a simple carving of the Chi-Rho, the first two letters of Christos, Christ's name in Greek. This was a popular Christian symbol in the days of early Christianity. Now if you will follow me …"

They guide moved off down one of the corridors, the tourists filing behind her. Father De Sanctis stood by Remi, not moving, so Remi made a move as if to follow the tour.

That's when Daniel flipped open the circuit box, pulled a heavy steel flashlight out of his pocket, and smashed the connection.

The entire catacombs were plunged into darkness.

CHAPTER THREE

Remi ducked to the side then to the left, down the darkened passageway that led to the Chapel of the Four Gospel Evangelists. She misjudged a bit, slammed her shoulder against the wall, then straightened out, running as fast as she dared, totally blind. She put out her hands to the side, running them along both walls so as not to bump into one again. She had to hope no barrier that wasn't on the map stood before her.

She also had to hope that the sound of running feet behind her was Daniel and not someone else.

Remi could barely hear whoever it was over the startled shouts of the rest of the tour.

Poor little Anke van der Berg. All she wanted to do was make a little extra money to fund her studies.

Suddenly, some light shone behind her, enough to faintly illuminate the tunnel ahead. She slowed, turned, and saw Daniel right behind her, so close that he bumped into her.

Remi stumbled, then looked to see that their tour guide, now fifty meters away, had turned on a flashlight and was shining it at the startled faces around her.

"What happened?" she said.

A babble of voices in reply. Then another flashlight turned on, shining right at them.

"There they are!" Father De Sanctis shouted.

Remi and Daniel ran.

Their pursuers' own lights helped them. A trio of flashlights illuminated enough of the corridor in front of them that they didn't have to pull out their own flashlights. Far behind, echoing through the stone tunnel over the sound of pursuing footsteps, they could hear that poor graduate student shouting.

"Don't leave the tour! You have to stay with the tour or you might get lost! Some of the tunnels are unstable!"

Neither the FBI agents nor the members of the Society of Devout Students paid her any attention.

As they ran, Remi noticed a couple of side chambers for tombs. A few of these were nothing more than niches for the bodies of poorer Christians in those early days. Others were rooms, decorated in a simple manner to commemorate the dead. None contained skeletons. This was not like the catacombs of Paris with their heaps of bones, some clad in moldering clothing of centuries gone by. The Parisian undercity used to fascinate her as a teenager.

Remi didn't have time for sightseeing anyway. Their rivals were right behind them, hoping to grab the prize she had pursued for so long.

She felt guilty, not only for scaring the other tourists and potentially getting that graduate student in trouble, but also for disturbing a fragile archaeological site and doing what she next intended on doing—digging around the Chapel of the Four Gospel Evangelists, one of the best-preserved chapels in the Catacombs of St. Mark.

But she didn't feel too guilty. She had no idea what this shadowy group would do with the cryptex secret. While they hadn't resorted to violence to get what they wanted, she wouldn't put it past them. Even though she had helped stop a killer from murdering its members, they did not seem terribly grateful and she simply had no idea what the group's goals and intentions were beyond keeping a potentially explosive early gospel, that of Longinus, from the public eye.

Whatever they wanted with the cryptex secret, she knew they would keep it for themselves.

And that made her better than them. While she admitted pursuing it out of her own obsession, like Daniel joked, she was also doing it so she could reveal a centuries-old secret to the world.

A secret so well kept that even she had no clear idea what it involved.

Up ahead, the passageway forked. Branching off to the left and right. That gave them an opportunity. From their memorization of the map in the previous couple of days, they knew they had to take the righthand path, and that the passageway branched again shortly afterwards.

If they did this right, they could lose their pursuers.

Remi glanced over her shoulder. The three men were gaining on them.

She stumbled, caught herself by grabbing onto Daniel's shoulder, and kept her eyes on where she was going.

They ducked around the corner and immediately slammed into some sort of metal sign that bruised Remi's knee. It fell to the floor with a loud clatter.

Stumbling over it in the dark, Remi and Daniel bumped into each other, steadied themselves, and moved forward into the nearly pitch-black passageway.

Remi reached for the lefthand wall, groping along the cold stone for an opening. The sound of pursuing feet grew louder. Anke van der Berg's protests continued to echo down the ancient tunnels. Remi thought she caught something about her calling the police. Well, that was inevitable.

Remi found the gap that signaled the branching off of another corridor. She tugged on Daniel, who was already headed that direction. Good. He had memorized the archaeological report's map as thoroughly as she had.

A good thing too, because getting chased might just make her forget where she was going, and she didn't relish the thought of being lost in an ancient network of unstable tunnels.

They moved with hesitant steps into the Stygian darkness, holding hands while she felt along the lefthand wall and he felt along the right. After a moment he tugged her to the right where, they both remembered, ran a narrow corridor with several small niches.

It was cold here, made colder still by the instinctive dread of darkness and dead places. Remi's hand left the wall, brushing nothing but air, before connecting with the wall again. That was the first niche. She kept her eyes wide, seeing nothing but not daring to close them. Again her hand lost the wall. She extended her arm, fingers straining, and slapped the edge of the wall again. That had been the second niche.

They needed the third.

They walked. And walked. Sounds of pursuit. Voices. The faintest of lights glimmering behind them as flashlights probed the darkness, searching.

Where was that third niche on the left??

Doubt nearly overwhelmed her. She must have forgotten. The stress of the chase and this creepy situation had made her forget the way.

They would be lost, wandering for ages in these tunnels until the Society of Devout Students found them.

Or the police found them.

There it was! The empty space she had been praying for. She tugged on Daniel so hard he bumped into her. The running steps drew nearer, the wavering light more distinct and yet still not enough to see by. Remi and Daniel moved diagonally across empty space and brushed against a doorway. They moved in, feeling all around them, and found that this room was as the map showed, with a little side room that would hide them from view from anyone passing by.

They felt along the walls, their fingers making the crumbling stone come off in little cascades that sounded like avalanches in the quiet corridors.

Quiet? Yes. The three men from the Society of Devout Students had stopped running.

They had stopped, and were no doubt standing still, listening for them.

Their flashlights remained a faint glimmer, the increase and decrease in light as they moved the beams around barely discernible.

Remi and Daniel moved their fingers gingerly now, probing for the little side niche the map told them was there. They couldn't stay in their present position. If the men passed by, they would be directly visible from the doorway. The little side niche was right next to the doorway, and judging from the map, invisible unless one actually entered the room.

There! They eased into it, Remi grimacing as their shoes crunched rubble underfoot. One of them, Remi wasn't sure who, kicked a little stone that clattered along the floor and struck the wall.

The sound of footsteps resumed. She and her partner used that to mask the sound of them fully retreating into the little cubbyhole. Remi tried to control her breathing, which sounded far too loud in the confined space.

Muttered voices. A distant shout. Their guide? She must have checked out the control box by now and seen it was hopelessly broken. Remi still couldn't believe that Daniel, an FBI agent with years of experience, would deliberately commit vandalism and criminal trespass.

But she had heard stories about him from other agents, mirthfully spread rumors in the cafeteria about how he had roughed up suspects, broken into houses without a warrant, broken a hundred rules and regulations to solve a case. None of the agents had criticized him, as all of these things had been done when he felt sure the suspect was guilty or a crime was about to be committed, but if any of these rumors were true, it could cost him his job.

Perhaps the FBI administration suspected these things were true and, not being able to prove them, had demoted him to the new and underfunded Antiquities Division. When she first met him he certainly seemed to feel he had been demoted.

How little she knew this strange, driven man pressed up against her in this confined space, their breath mingling in the cool, dead air.

The footsteps and muttering stopped. Both sides listened for signs of the other.

The footsteps resumed, and Remi cringed as she saw the light gradually grow brighter.

The room they had hidden in gradually came into view. It was a side tomb just like the others, with shelves cut into the stone walls in which to put the skeletons, now thankfully long gone. The stone slabs that had once covered them up had also disappeared. Remi knew that these bore inscriptions and simple artwork, done by amateur hands since the Christians didn't dare hire professionals who might inform the authorities. Those slabs, depending on when they had been removed, were now in private collections or museums.

The little niche by the door that they hid in had once held a more ornate tomb, probably with a sarcophagus. That, too, had disappeared, giving them a place to hide. Odd to think that a long-ago grave robbery might save their mission.

Or maybe their lives.

The footsteps drew closer. The lights grew brighter.

Then the men paused again. They must have stopped at the intersection, just beyond where Remi and Daniel had slammed into that warning sign. The memory prompted Remi to look at the ceiling. Even in the feeble light she could see several deep cracks.

The footsteps became louder. Remi winced as the light waxed, then a beam shone directly into the room in which they hid.

The beam searched every corner of the room, then moved away.

Remi had to suppress a sigh of relief. The trick had worked! They hadn't seen the side niche!

The footsteps withdrew, the lights growing dimmer. Remi felt safe enough to breathe again.

Until they returned, running.

Remi braced for an attack. Daniel shifted to get in front of her.

The three men from the Society of Devout Students ran right past their crypt and away.

Perfect. They had run along this passageway, looked in all the side crypts, not found them, and assumed she and Daniel had taken the other passage. Now they'd be searching that one for a fair bit of time, assuming she and Daniel had gotten a good head start.

Luckily, that wasn't the right way to go to get to the chapel. This passage was.

"Come on," she whispered so softly she could barely hear herself.

Daniel didn't say a word, only moved out of the niche to stand in the crypt, the last of the diminishing light fading away until darkness swallowed him.

Remi moved out, lifting her feet high so as not to knock any stones again.

A tiny light appeared before her. Daniel had turned on his flashlight but held his hand over it, only a little pinprick point shining through his fingers.

"Old FBI trick," he whispered.

Remi smiled. Although she was getting top marks in her accelerated training, she still had a lot to learn.

They headed out, Daniel leading with his little light shining on the ground before them so they wouldn't knock anything and make a noise. Remi kept glancing back and was relieved to see their pursuers' light had vanished completely and Daniel's light did not penetrate the darkness behind them.

She and her partner walked without speaking along the narrow passageway. Its roof was arched, but Remi could see several spots where the stones had slipped. Piles of rubble on the ground spoke of minor cave-ins. That sign they had blundered into had spoken the truth. This seventeen-hundred-year-old tunnel really was unstable.

They passed a couple of preserved tombs, the facing stones still on them, the skeletons no doubt still lying in their niches. These had been carved in the Roman style, with the mournful faces of their long-lost residents staring out at them in bas-relief.

Despite all her training, despite what she liked to think of as her academic detachment, Remi shuddered.

Daniel's covered flashlight gave so little light they looked just as real as he did.

The turn of the tunnel came up abruptly. Remi jerked and stopped short. She had known this turn was coming, but she had been so distracted by the faces it caught her by surprise.

Daniel gestured to the left. Remi took a deep breath and nodded, unsure if he even saw the gesture.

They turned to the left, and there, just a few steps beyond, the tunnel opened up to the Chapel of the Four Gospel Evangelists.

Remi stopped and gasped, her awe echoing softly down the ancient passageways.

CHAPTER FOUR

She beheld a masterpiece of Early Christian art.

Of course she had seen the chapel in photographs. She had studied the dry archaeological reports, the discussion in art history journals, but nothing could express the experience of seeing it firsthand.

Remi felt more than saw the chamber open up into the largest space they had yet seen since entering the catacombs. The pinprick of light Daniel let through his fingers barely showed a large rectangular room about ten meters on its longest side, with a low vaulted ceiling. On this ceiling was a fresco that had somehow remained remarkably preserved over the centuries.

Daniel played his light over it, and as he did his fingers unconsciously opened up a little to allow them to see this priceless work of art more clearly.

A large, winged lion, the symbol of St. Mark, took up much of the ceiling. It was trampling a serpent, the symbol of the Devil, under its paws while its jaws were open for a silent roar. In front of the lion was painted a family—a man and woman and three children—with arms upraised in prayer.

The entire scene was done with a simple, expressive mastery that was far superior to most art found in this or any other of the early catacombs.

Remi and Daniel stood staring for a moment. While several cracks ran along the ceiling, no chunks of plaster had fallen away like in so many other early Christian paintings hidden beneath the Appian Way. Her expert eye looked for signs that it had been restored and saw none. It remained in its original state.

It's a miracle that it had remained so well preserved, Remi thought. *The very painting that looks over the next secret to the cryptex.*

Of course that was just a coincidence, she told herself, and the cryptex was deposited here centuries after the fresco was painted. Academics do not talk about miracles.

And yet she could not shake the feeling that the cryptex had preserved it somehow.

A distant echo snapped Remi back into a more practical frame of mind.

It snapped Daniel out of it too. He put his fingers over the flashlight again, reducing the light to almost nothing.

"The altar," Remi whispered.

He probed the walls with the light, passing over open niches where skeletons once lay until, on the far wall, the beam rested on a stone platform cut out of the rock. It stood waist high, rectangular, not unlike the Roman pagan altars of the time except for there being no writing or carvings on it. From what she knew from the rare depictions of worship from those times, the altar would have been covered with a cloth as well as a chalice and plate for the Communion.

Daniel shone his light beyond the altar and there on the wall, as well preserved as the painting on the ceiling, was a full-sized portrait of Jesus Christ.

He wore a white toga like the Romans of his day, one hand raised with two fingers extended in a sign of blessing. His features were Mediterranean, with olive skin and eyes and hair dark. He seemed to look at them with a calm gaze. Remi shivered.

Another echo, louder this time. Without a word they moved for the altar.

Remi peered at the details of the painting in the dim light, remembering what the fresco at the Monastery of St. Pishoy had hinted at.

The blessing fingers of Christ revealing a great secret. In the Coptic mural it had been a book, no doubt the Gospels, and here it would be … what?

She ran her hand along the plastered surface before coming to bare stone. The wall felt rough under her fingers. Whoever had excavated this chapel out of solid rock had not taken the time to smooth down the surface.

Every centimeter, she pressed against the wall, moving her hand up and down a little to take in all the space that Christ was blessing. The problem was, there was a good two meters of wall before she reached the corner, and more echoes reverberated down the passageway as she searched.

Would the men from the Society of Devout Students really be that noisy, or had the police arrived so soon?

She wasn't even sure how long they had been down here. This place, with its lack of light or contact with the surface, seemed timeless.

"Where is it?" Daniel whispered. "We need to get going."

Remi didn't respond. She had been over the entire surface now and hadn't found a thing. She was assuming a bump in the stone would open a hidden shelf, like in the Church of Saint Pantaleon of Nicomedia in Italy, where she had found a little ceramic statue of the Virgin Mary containing her next clue.

But here she found nothing.

She began to run her hands along the space a second time, moving further up and down. Where was it?

Then she paused, remembering the painting at the monastery again.

A man had been holding the book in that painting. Had Christ been blessing the man and not the book?

She looked to her left. One of the empty niches was at the exact same level as Christ's fingers.

Her heart sank. That niche had been cleared out ages ago. If the next clue had been hidden inside, it was long gone.

She rushed over to it, tears in her eyes. Daniel's light followed her, approaching footsteps filling her ears.

There was nothing in it but dust.

The footsteps drew closer. Daniel switched off the light.

No! It's got to be here!

Blindly she reached out, feeling with her hands along the sides of the niche, the confines that once held the mortal remains of one of the first Christians in the world.

Please ...

Her fingers passed over a bump on the side of the niche. She moved her fingers back and ran them all over it, using a fingernail to trace its circumference.

There was a seam running all around the knob. She could feel it.

Putting several fingers on the knob, she pressed with all her might.

A loud click echoed through the catacombs. Daniel took in a soft intake of breath. Remi winced.

The footsteps stopped.

Groping around in the dark, she found that a small portion of the wall had opened up, just like in the Church of Saint Pantaleon of Nicomedia.

She pulled on it, and the stone grinding on stone made another noise so loud that she gritted her teeth.

She froze. What was that? The sound of soft movement? She couldn't be sure.

Reaching inside the niche, she felt around the tiny space and, at the bottom, her hands rested on something cool. Metal. Round. A coin? It seemed too big for that. She grabbed it and felt around more. Nothing else.

She ached to ask Daniel to turn on the light so she could double check, but that would be foolish.

Foolish? This whole thing was foolish! What was she, a famous academic and trainee agent for the FBI, doing breaking into ancient sites and stealing treasure? And why in the world would Daniel help her?

She didn't really understand this man in the darkness next to her, any more than she truly understood herself.

All she knew was that she needed to do this, and Daniel, for whatever reasons of his own, felt compelled to help.

She turned, reaching out in the blackness for Daniel until her fingertips brushed his chest. Remi moved in closer, whispered in his ear.

"I got it."

A little sound. Him smiling? Did smiling make a noise? With no other senses to go by, maybe you really could hear a friend smile.

"Let's get out of here," he whispered back. "We can make it a little way without the light."

Remi nodded before realizing how useless that gesture was. She smiled, felt around for his hand, and took it. It struck her that this intimate gesture should bother her, but it didn't. Holding hands was the only way to stay together in the complete darkness, after all. But did they really have to interlock their fingers?

Together they moved for the doorway, reaching out with their free hands to find the wall.

They had misjudged slightly and missed the door. Finding it a moment later, they stepped out into the passageway …

… and got blinded as three flashlight beams turned on and shone right in their faces.

A low chuckle. Father De Sanctis's voice came to them from beyond the glare.

"I told you that you aren't as clever as you think you are."

Daniel got between them and Remi.

"Buzz off. We got here first."

"I fail to see the significance of that statement," the priest replied.

A beam focused on Remi's hand, glinting off the metal. Remi couldn't resist the opportunity to study what she had found. It looked like a brass medallion of some kind with complex designs. Remi quickly put it behind her back, memories of getting caught smoking in her high school bathroom popping into her head.

"Hand it over," came another voice. Deeper, more stern.

"No," Remi said.

She wished she could have said it more firmly. Instead, the word came out as a warble, a good two octaves higher than she intended.

"That is Church property," Father De Sanctis said.

"Oh, so you're going to hand it over to the proper authorities?" Daniel said, sarcasm lacing his voice. He was more accustomed to danger and had never been through a Catholic upbringing. Remi could feel herself blush just hearing him speak to a priest like that.

"We *are* the proper authorities."

"Like hell you are," Daniel grumbled.

A flashlight shifted. One of the men stepped forward. A hand reached out of the darkness and into the light.

"Give it to me," a low voice growled.

Suddenly, Daniel flicked on his flashlight right in the man's face. He grunted, stepped back, momentarily blinded.

"Run!" Daniel shouted.

Remi turned and bolted, pulling out her own flashlight and flicking it on as she hurried down the passageway.

After a few steps, sounds of a struggle behind her made her stop. All she could make out was swirling flashlights and shadowy figures darting around several paces behind. A flash of light passed over Daniel's face.

"Move it!" Daniel shouted.

She ran, stumbling over a heap of rubble and nearly falling before she recovered at the last moment. A modern stairway leading up to an emergency exit lay not far ahead. If she could get out, lose herself in the countryside, she could keep this medallion or whatever it was away from the Society of Devout Students.

But what about Daniel? What were they doing to him back there?

The sound of pursuing feet made her pick up speed, the beam of her flashlight dancing crazily in time to her steps.

The footsteps drew closer. They must have overpowered Daniel and were now coming after her. She knew she couldn't fight them off. Her only choice was to run.

She didn't look over her shoulder. She put all her energy into running. Into getting away.

A sick feeling in the pit of her stomach told her that she wouldn't.

CHAPTER FIVE

The footsteps had almost caught up now, echoing loudly in her ears. Heavy breathing made her think of a wolf pursuing her in the forest. She had always found the story of Little Red Riding Hood terrifying.

"Leave me alone!" she shouted.

"That's a hell of a thank you for all the things I've done for you," Daniel huffed behind her.

"What happened to them?"

"Pushed them all in a big heap. They aren't far behind."

"You pushed a priest?" Remi said, laughing.

"You pepper sprayed one!"

They rounded a corner and Remi took the opportunity to glance back. They were barely ten meters behind.

She picked up speed. Her flashlight caught the metal staircase at the end of the passageway.

They made it as someone shouted behind them. Flashlight beams focused on their desperate bid for escape.

Up the clattering steps, poorly built and shaking under their pounding feet. Dust trickled down from the ceiling to powder their hair.

Remi hit the push bar on one of the double doors like an American football player smashing into a member of the other team. She supposed there was a term for that but she didn't know it and didn't care. All she wanted was to get out.

The door flew open and daylight jabbed her eyes.

Daniel burst out a moment later, nearly bowling her over. He spun and slammed the door shut, then leaned on them both as they bucked as the men chasing them tried to smash through.

Daniel planted his feet further apart. The doors bucked again, harder this time.

Remi looked around. The doors were on the side of a small brick structure built to house the top of the staircase and nothing more. She saw no way to lock it from the outside. No doubt it was a one-way door allowing people out in case of an emergency, but not allowing people to sneak in.

The doors bucked again, so much she could see the enraged faces on the other side. It was three against one. Daniel couldn't hold them off forever.

"Find something to block the doors!" Daniel shouted.

The little structure stood at the edge of one of the farmer's fields, cordoned off with a bit of barbed wire to keep the animals away. She saw nothing around to block the door with. At least there were no people in sight.

There! A stack of bricks by the wall. She grabbed one and shoved it between the door handles.

The doors bucked again, but this time they barely moved.

Daniel laughed and turned to her. Remi rushed into his arms, laughing with delight and triumph.

"We did it! We did it!"

They held each other tight.

A bang on the door snapped her out of it and she realized what she was doing.

What *they* were doing, because he hadn't let go either.

She looked up at him. For a long moment, barely a second but long enough, neither moved.

Remi stepped away first. "We need to get out of here before they knock that brick loose."

They were already trying. One of them was jerking the door back and forth. The brick jerked, slowly edging its way out from the handles.

Remi shoved it back into place to buy themselves more time and they ran off to find a way through the hedge and back onto the Appian Way. They needed to get well away before those three made it out, and before the police showed up.

Because if they got caught red-handed, both of them would be out of a job.

They skirted the edge of a field for about half a kilometer, checking over their shoulders constantly for pursuit. Their luck held and no one saw them. At last they came close to where Daniel's phone told them stood another bus stop.

Stopping to catch their breath and rearrange their clothes so it didn't look like they had just been in a fight in a set of ancient Roman catacombs, they pushed through the hedge again …

… and right into a crowd of tourists.

The same crowd of tourists who had spotted them coming through the hedge the last time.

One of them whistled. Several of them laughed. The Englishman who had teased them before called out, "Couldn't wait for another go, eh?"

Blushing from her scalp to her toes, Remi got in line for the bus. She still had enough presence of mind to check around for the police or Father De Sanctis and his priestly goons. Luckily, neither made an appearance before the bus showed up

They had gotten away, but we now faced with a deeper mystery, and a case waiting for them back in the United States.

* * *

Sitting on the plane back to Washington, D.C., Remi knew she should get some sleep, but she also knew sleep was impossible.

Not as long as she had this strange puzzle in her hand, a puzzle that had been hidden in the catacombs for centuries.

It was a circular medallion of brass, five centimeters or two inches in diameter. The back side was flat and blank. The front side was slightly convex and inscribed with strange, meandering lines that looked unlike any style of art she had ever seen. A small raised boss in the center was unornamented, although all the lines ended at it.

If she hadn't found it in a hidden shelf in an ancient tomb, she would have thought it was some New Age medallion from the Sixties.

But perhaps she shouldn't call it a medallion. It didn't have a hole through which to suspend it from a cord or a chain. As for the designs, she had no idea what they could signify.

Daniel, sitting next to her, reached over and took the medallion. Instinctively Remi tightened her grip, then let go a moment later. A flicker of a smile passed over Daniel's face. Remi flushed. He had noticed. Hopefully he'd realize that had been only an automatic reaction and not a sign of mistrust.

Because she did trust this driven, private man. While a bit of a barbarian, he had his own code of honor and deeply loyal to his friends.

"What do you make of this?" Daniel asked, turning the medallion this way and that in the dim light. He kept his voice down. The men who had chased them weren't on this flight—Daniel had checked—but it paid to be careful.

"I have no idea," Remi admitted, keeping her own voice low.

"Maybe a map? It kind of looks like the elevation lines in a topo map."

"Except the mural was painted in the ninth century. They didn't have topo maps back then."

"Maybe, maybe not. There's a lot we don't know about the ancient world. Look at the Antikythera mechanism. No one suspected that existed until it was discovered."

"Actually the Classical texts talk about experimental steam engines and other mechanical devices, but you're right. We had no idea how advanced the Greeks had become. So perhaps it could be some sort of topographic map, or maybe a stylized map or drawing. I'll just keep looking at it every now and then, hoping the answer will come to me like when I stared at the photos of the Coptic mural."

"Stare while you have the chance. Assistant Director Ochiai is dumping us with a case as soon as we get back."

Remi grimaced and looked back at the medallion, or whatever it was. Usually the prospect of a case got her excited. Not this time. Now it would interfere with her investigation of the latest clue in her hunt for the cryptex mystery. She had thought that actually finding and opening the cryptex would be the end, but it had turned out to be only the beginning.

She had to get to the next step, and quickly. Father De Sanctis and his organization knew she had it, and would be doing everything in their power to get it. And they might not even need to get it. They had a massive library and archives at their disposal, and might be able to figure out the next step without the medallion. She wasn't sure if that was possible, but she knew so little of their capabilities, or even what she herself was hunting, that she couldn't discount it as a threat.

Which meant she needed to figure out this medallion's secrets as quickly as possible.

Or all her hard work might be snatched away from her.

CHAPTER SIX

FBI Headquarters, Washington D.C., the next day

Daniel stifled a yawn as he and Remi sat down in Assistant Director Ochiai's office.

"Sorry to cut your vacation short," she said. "Would you like some coffee?"

"That would be lovely, thank you," Remi said as she sat down beside Daniel.

The assistant director moved over to the side of the office, under a black and white photo of Japanese-American cowboys branding a steer somewhere in Texas, and started up the espresso machine that sat on a small side table.

"Is that a new one?" Daniel asked, pointing to a photo of a man who he knew was the assistant director's cousin wrestling a steer to the ground. Man and bovine had their faces pressed together.

"New and old," she replied, brewing up the coffee. "I took this a couple of years ago but only got around to printing and framing it last week. My FBI work keeps me from my hobbies."

Daniel shrugged. He didn't have any hobbies.

Remi's brow furrowed as she looked more closely at the photo. "Is he … biting the steer on the lip?"

Assistant Director Ochiai laughed. "He is. It's called bulldogging, invented by an African-American cowboy named Bill Pickett back around the turn of the last century. It's a good way to make the steer submit to you and get it on the ground."

Remi looked horrified. Daniel laughed.

"Why in the world would someone do that?" Remi gasped.

"It shows courage and self-control, two traits that cowboys respect, the same as FBI agents," the assistant director replied. "You're not a vegetarian, are you?"

"No," Remi replied.

"She might become one," Daniel said with a grin.

The assistant director brought over two steaming cups of espresso. Daniel was surprised at how much she had warmed up in the past few months. Perhaps she felt a shift to the Antiquities Division had been a demotion, just like Daniel had felt. But after several important cases, all solved thanks to the two agents sitting in front of her, perhaps she had reassessed.

She sat back behind her desk, serious again. She handed over a folder. Daniel took it and saw a crime scene.

"His name is Michael Grayson, a multimillionaire from old money," his boss said. "Stocks. Bonds. Real estate. His father collected antiquities after the war, when buying was cheap and regulation light. The son carried on the family tradition."

"Including the light regulation?" Daniel asked, passing by a printout and flipping through the photos. It showed a trim man in his early seventies lying on a Persian carpet, his head ravaged by numerous blows from a blunt object. He wore a night gown and slippers, and obviously had not been expecting guests. A stranger, then? Or someone close enough that Grayson didn't feel the need to dress up? Family or a servant, maybe?

The assistant director went on.

"That's something I'd like you to investigate. So far we have no evidence that he was dealing in illegal antiquities. There has never been an accusation or investigation. An initial check by the local police did not find anything stolen."

Daniel raised an eyebrow. There must have been something. Maybe something Grayson didn't put in one of those open shelves and display cases he saw in the background of so many photographs. The place sure was a mess. The killer had been searching for something, that was for sure. Maybe he didn't find it?

He flipped to another photo and came on a squat Hispanic woman in a maid's uniform, clubbed to death just like her employer.

"Who's the maid?" he asked.

"Valentina Montero. Age 52. According to her husband she left home at the usual time in order to start her shift at 5:30 in the morning. The other staff say she was always punctual. The coroner gave the time for her death at about that hour. Interestingly, Michael Grayson was killed approximately two hours before."

"So our man was searching the collection for two whole hours when the maid showed up," Daniel said.

"I've heard of the Grayson collection," Remi said. "It's vast, one of the most extensive collections in the United States. It would probably take more than two hours to search through if you didn't know where a particular object was stored. And there were actually three generations of collectors. They collected widely, everything from ancient Egyptian art to Shaker furniture."

"Then we have a lot to look through," Daniel said, draining his coffee and standing up. Remi followed suit. "We'll read the file on the way down to the mansion."

"Glad to have you back," Assistant Director Ochiai said, "and I apologize for pulling you out of Italy at a moment's notice. Once this is all over you can apply for your respective vacations."

Daniel tensed. He had noted the phrase "*respective* vacations," said casually and without any emphasis.

But the meaning was clear, he thought as they walked out of the office and down the hallway. Ochiai knew they had gone to Italy together. Did she suspect they were up to something? Or did she think they had gone on vacation for, um, personal reasons?

Well, thinking that was better than her knowing the truth. It's not every day that a pair of FBI agents steal a medallion covered in cryptic, seemingly abstract carvings that were no doubt a code leading … somewhere.

He should have had his head examined for pulling off a stunt like that, and yet he didn't feel guilty. Well, at least not too guilty. Remi was onto something, something the Church wanted to cover up, and the Church had covered up far too much already. They had allowed predators free access to children, just like his mother had allowed her boyfriend free access to him.

Taking away something the Church had no right to claim seemed poetic justice.

Plus he couldn't leave Remi to do it alone. She was too impulsive, too single-minded. While brilliant, she needed a partner with experience and perspective.

Besides, she was really good company, and getting away from the States to go on a crazy adventure had been a welcome break from him and his ex-wife Veronica trying to pick up the pieces and build a relationship again.

Finding an ancient artifact hidden in the catacombs outside Rome was a hell of a lot easier than that.

* * *

The drive did not take long. As Daniel sat at the wheel, thinking over the new case in his mind, Remi read through the slim file.

"Not much in here," Remi said. "No criminal investigations. Widowered with no known romantic entanglements. No known enemies."

"Someone that rich always has enemies," Daniel replied. They had left the highway ten minutes before and were in fairly open countryside with woods and fields punctuated by mansions.

"Perhaps. It's interesting that the killer had two hours of free access to the collection and didn't steal any one of a thousand priceless artifacts. He could have taken literally millions of dollars' worth of antiquities."

"He must have gone for something very specific. But he also might have had more than two hours. You're assuming he killed Grayson right away. He, or she, might have grilled the old guy. Maybe tortured him."

"The coroner's report said there were no signs of torture."

"Not all torture is physical," Daniel said in a quiet voice.

"Well, if the killer did torture Grayson, he didn't get any information out of him. These pictures make it look like the house had been hit by a whirlwind."

Daniel turned into an open ironwork gate. A police officer stood next to it. They showed their ID and drove up a long curving drive to stop in front of an elaborate mansion of the kind millionaires made in the late nineteenth century in imitation of European castles. The thing even had turrets and fake battlements guarding the gabled roof. Even under a bright autumn day with the Potomac River glittering in the background, the place looked gloomy.

A stooped and balding older man in a trench coat came out of the front door and shambled down the flight of marble steps.

"You must be the FBI agents," he said. "I'm Detective Foster, homicide. We have all the employees here for questioning as you requested. One employee is missing. Donald Willis, the groundskeeper and overall fix-it man. Not answering his phone. Hasn't been to work since the time of the murders. We've launched a manhunt. We've also set out all the purchase records for you to study. Grayson kept everything in files."

"What did you find when you searched Willis's residence?"

"Looks like some clothes are missing and there's no suitcase in the house. Nothing of value found in the house. Law enforcement in this state and all surrounding states are on alert. We'll get him."

"Good. Maybe we can wrap this whole thing up quickly," Daniel said. "Remi, why don't you look at those records while I talk to the staff."

"All right," Remi said, looking eager. Daniel smiled. She loved this stuff.

"There are no security cameras in the building," the detective said, "simply a key code on the gate and a burglar alarm. No real security at all. Surprising considering how much stuff he's got in the house."

"Not so surprising," Daniel said. "I've seen it before in rich houses. They think their wealth keeps them safe. So the burglar alarm didn't go off?"

"Nope. It's linked to a local security company. They didn't receive any alarms and the system shows no signs of tampering."

"Interesting."

The three of them entered a grand entrance hall with a huge chandelier and a sweeping staircase leading upstairs. Old paintings hung on the walls. A suit of armor clutching a halberd stood at the base of the stairs.

Detective Foster pointed to a hallway on the left. "Second door on the right is a study. The records and receipts are all on the desk."

Remi nodded and hurried off. Daniel continued with the detective to a room just to the right of the staircase. It looked like a mixture of a library and exhibition room, and remarkable for both. Daniel ignored the small group of people gathered there to spend a moment taking it all in.

The room was lined with oak bookshelves filled with what Daniel knew were rare books. His mother had been an historian, and so he had grown up around old leather-bound tomes, and even older ones bound in vellum with their titles handwritten in cursive on the spine with quill pens. He saw plenty of examples of those on the shelves.

Between the shelves stood display cases with antiquities on the theme of books and reading. He made a slow circle of the room, ignoring the nervous-looking staff. Let them stew a bit. Made the questioning easier once he came to it.

Incredible stuff. An ancient Egyptian papyrus with figures of animal-headed gods and the giant serpent of the underworld. An example of early Chinese block printing. Some clay containers from Uruk with simple pictograms incised onto them. One was broken open and several little clay tokens sat next to it, matching the pictograms on the outer shell.

He was looking at the origins of writing.

Almost six thousand years ago, before the invention of cuneiform, some of the early city-states in what is now Iraq developed a simple way of tallying trade goods. You made little tokens of sheep or bushels of wheat or whatever it was you were selling, and sealed them inside a clay ball with the same number of symbols incised on the outside. It worked as sort of a certified letter to the person at the other end of the exchange. These simple word pictures eventually developed into more abstract shapes and ideas and ended up as cuneiform.

Early examples such as these were incredibly rare and, Daniel assumed, incredibly expensive.

Interestingly, none of the books or display cases in this room had been disturbed.

Guess our killer isn't much of a reader.

Daniel spun on the assembled staff members, the suddenness of his action making them jerk. He smiled inwardly.

Four people stood there, two women and two men. He stared at each one slowly.

The first was a slim, erect man dressed as a butler, with a shiny scalp atop a fringe of graying hair. The second was a portly man in a chef's white clothing. A red nose and rosy cheeks spoke of just as much wine going into his mouth as into the beef stew. The next staff member was dressed as a cleaning lady, much like her unlucky coworker. The fourth was a woman in her thirties in business attire and a calm air. She was the only one who met his eye.

"I take it you're the personal secretary."

"Yes. I gave all the records over to Detective Foster," she said, nodding toward the detective, who stood in the doorway, hanging back while also blocking any escape. The detective knew some psychological tricks of his own. Always nice to work with professionals.

"Did Grayson make any large purchases lately?"

"He makes large purchases on a regular basis."

"Did he deal with anyone new recently?"

"No."

Daniel's gaze swept down the line. "So when are you all supposed to get into work?"

It was the butler who spoke, and when he did it was with an English accent. Daniel had seen this before in rich households. The East Coast American wealthy loved England, so they employed a little bit of it to serve them drinks.

"Mrs. Montero comes in first at 5:30. Mr. Grayson likes, um, *liked* quiet mornings. So Ms. Winston would come in at nine along with myself. The chef would only come in at eleven, and the afternoon maid, Mrs. Jackson, comes in at 2 pm and stays until ten, at which point I also leave."

"No one stays here full time?"

"No. Mr. Grayson likes privacy and quiet."

"And what time does the groundskeeper come in?" Daniel asked, noticing the glaring omission.

The butler scowled. "Any time he liked. He was most slovenly with his personal habits and punctuality."

"Personal habits?"

"Drunk while on duty," the butler said, casting a sidelong glance at the chef, who seemed unphased. "Poorly dressed. Tromping through the house in muddy work boots. He acted like the lord of the manor."

"Why did Mr. Grayson tolerate that?"

The butler gave a little shrug. "He was good at his job, I'll give him that. Kept the garden in good order and promptly fixed anything that needed fixing around the house. But he didn't know his place."

Daniel frowned. If the groundskeeper wasn't the prime suspect in a murder case he'd be taking his side over the butler's. He didn't think people should have a “place.” He’d been given a “place” once and didn’t like it one bit.

Just for that, he was going to stay here and grill these people, the butler especially. He had a lot of questions, mostly ones the detective had already asked, but he had learned from years of experience that when people are asked the same question several times, the answers started to take on some interesting and revealing variations.

But he didn’t hold out much hope for anything big. It was the groundskeeper they needed to hunt down. He was the one missing.

And yet nothing of value was missing.

Or was there?

One of them might be in on it. They were all intimately familiar with the house and collection, after all.

He decided to ask Detective Foster to get a court order to open the groundskeeper’s emails. Considering that Willis was an obvious flight risk, the judge would fast track it. They should have a response within a few hours.

In the meantime, he’d grill this crew. That would give Remi a chance to look through the records. He had a feeling she’d find something there almost as interesting as what was in Willis’s emails.

CHAPTER SEVEN

Remi had been studying Grayson's purchase records for two hours and seen all that she needed to see.

The man had been buying illegal antiquities.

Not all the time, but if he couldn't get something via legal means, he got it illegally.

So common. The art world was filled with people like him.

Even though she knew this, finding yet another culprit always made her feel a bit betrayed. She had gone into history and art with the innocence and eagerness borne of a lifetime of enthusiasm, and it had taken some time for her childlike awe of collectors and esteemed academics to wear off.

It began to wear off in university, with professors old enough to be her father or even grandfather making passes at her. She knew from other students that this happened in every department, but for some silly reason she had not expected it to happen with art historians.

Then her eyes began to see more clearly. The snobbery when they learned she was from the middle class. The bickering. The petty infighting. The undignified scramble for funding. If it wasn't for a few truly good professors and her untarnished love for the subject, she would have quit.

That and the fact that there was nowhere else to go. The other departments were just as bad. She had dated an archaeology student for a while who had a thousand horror stories about his department.

So she went on, gritting her teeth through all the pettiness and drama, resigning herself to the fact that the field was filled with martinets and outright fraudsters and thieves, and yet still to the present day she had managed to preserve some level of unconscious innocence that made every new revelation of this sort a disappointment.

Daniel came in.

"How's it going?" he asked.

"He was buying illegal antiquities."

"Surprise. Surprise. Can you prove it?"

"Oh yes. The pieces all have authentication and provenance papers, but some of these are forged. Take this one here, for a Late Roman *terra sigillata* lamp. It was verified by Professor Weston. The signature looks correct, but it says he was at the University of Southhampton. He wasn't that year. He was supposed to stay on but he got an offer from the University of Twente in the Netherlands and left early. Not many people knew that until after he had already left, so the forger made a mistake."

"But the signature looks good?"

"Oh yes, the forgeries are good. I've found a few other inconsistencies. Nothing a government official would catch, only a specialist with years of experience who actually knows the academics and departments involved. One or two of the customs stamps also looked forged, but we'd need an expert to make sure."

"Good start. Find anything missing from the collection? Anything newly purchased that hadn't been put on display?"

"No. There's a box of new acquisitions from Sotheby's. Legal things. They're all accounted for. Everything else was marked "displayed." He kept very thorough records for a man committing a crime."

Daniel grunted. "The immunity of the wealthy. Anyway, Detective Foster just got access to Donald Willis's Gmail records. Let's see if Mr. Fix-it was up to no good. He's set up in another room."

Remi got up and Daniel led her to a reading room lined with books and early medieval woodblock prints, each worth tens of thousands, and found Detective Foster seated at a Louis XIV desk with ornamentation in gold leaf. The MacBook Air he was working on looked as out of place as a UFO resting on top of Stonehenge.

"And we're in," he said triumphantly. "We already checked his phone records and got nothing. But I've found that criminals often think email is more secure. So let's see what we can see."

They looked over his shoulder as the detective ran through the emails of the last few days. Other than a few messages to a brother, and a receipt for a Netflix payment, there was nothing. He kept scrolling. Still nothing. In fact there were few emails at all.

Detective Foster opened up the trash folder, and came upon an email thread with someone who never signed a name. He only signed with the string of numbers he used as a username for his Proton Mail account.

"Proton Mail is a secure email server out of Switzerland," the detective said. "Out of bounds for us. Lots of criminals use it. Willis is apparently not smart enough to use it himself."

He opened the thread. It started the morning Grayson had been found dead.

Willis: "You still interested?"

Proton Mail User: "Sure."

Willis: "I got what you asked for. A good one. But I need to meet NOW."

Proton Mail User: "Can't. I'm on other business. How about in a few days?"

Willis: "You can't meet earlier?"

Proton Mail User: "No. It will keep."

Willis: "Not it won't. They'll find it's missing. And there's another problem. I can't talk about it other than to tell you it's serious."

Proton Mail User: "Whatever problem that is, it's yours. I'm out of town. The soonest I can do it is the 24th at 2pm at the old gas station."

That's today, Remi thought.

Willis: "I'll be there. Bring the money."

"Jesus, that's in fifteen minutes!" Daniel cried, looking at his watch. "Do you know what he means about an old gas station?"

Detective Foster thought for a moment, then his eyes lit up. "There's an abandoned gas station on McClellan Lane!"

"How far is it?"

The detective's face fell. "About fifteen minutes."

They were up and running within a heartbeat.

"We'll take our car," Daniel said. "It's unmarked."

"All right," Detective Foster said. "I'll get the patrolman here to stay and watch the place. I'll also have him radio in to see if any patrol cars are in the area. This is a pretty rural region, so don't get your hopes up."

"OK, but have them keep their distance. We want to take these guys by surprise."

"No problem."

After a brief consultation with the cop standing guard over the staff members, they ran out to Daniel's car and shot down a country lane, Detective Foster giving directions.

"It's a gas station that went out of business a few years back," the detective explained. "All boarded up. I'm going to take you down a gravel road that goes around back. We can sneak up on them."

"Sounds good," Remi said, heart beating fast. She checked her gun. Her training with it had only just begun. Her instructor said she was a natural, partially thanks to the training her policeman father had given her as a teen. She still didn't feel confident in a combat situation, though.

"Sounds like a good approach," Daniel said, "but if we're on this gravel road and they get away on the paved road in front of the gas station, how are we going to catch them?"

"The gravel road has access to the paved road one mile down the road each way. It's a risk, true, but we want to catch them in the act," Detective Foster replied.

"All right," Daniel said. He still didn't sound happy, though.

Neither was Remi. With no guarantee of backup, Willis might get away. But that was a risk they would have to take.

They got off the main road and sped down a gravel back road that didn't look like it got much use, speeding past farmer's fields and woodland. Remi checked her watch. It was time. One thing she had learned in her training was that criminals were extremely punctual when it came to deliveries and pickups. People who were late got their partners suspicious and nervous, and that could be unhealthy.

"Stop right here," Detective Foster said.

There was no shoulder, the road being hemmed in by light forest on both sides, so Daniel simply stopped in the middle of the road.

They got out and the detective pointed through the woods. As silently as they could, they moved into it. Remi noticed the trees here were young, with relatively thin trunks. She guessed it had been a famer's field perhaps a hundred or so years ago and then abandoned to nature. The trees would not give much cover, and neither would the thin underbrush.

Daniel and the detective took their guns out. Reluctantly, so did Remi.

They came upon the gas station quicker than she expected. Through the trees they could see a low building with cheap aluminum siding. They came on the back of the building, and could see little but a stack of old tires and a back door marked "toilet."

No, there was more. As they drew closer, they could see the back end of a car parked in front of the building. Willis's vehicle? Or the mysterious buyer's? And was the second vehicle not here yet or parked out of view?

They moved more slowly, trying to make the least amount of noise possible and yet eager to get there while they still had still time. Daniel gestured to Detective Foster, who moved to the right to cover that side of the building, then her partner looked at her, pointed to her and himself, and then to the side of the building where they could see the back of the car.

Remi's heart fluttered. She licked her lips, checked the safety was off on her gun, and followed.

She winced as she broke a twig underfoot. It sounded like a gunshot in the quiet forest, although the rational part of her mind told her it wasn't loud at all.

At least no one came tearing around the corner, guns blazing.

They got to the back wall and crept along it. Voices came to them from the other side of the building, too quiet to make out the words.

They got to the corner, Daniel taking the lead, a move required by the manual because of his senior rank but nonetheless annoying. He peeked around the corner and ducked back. Then Remi took a look.

A well-built, short man in his forties matching Wallis's description stood facing a tough-looking guy with beady eyes and an open leather jacket over leather pants. A motorcycle stood parked in front of the gas station. Both were partially turned away from the back of the building, no doubt keeping an eye on the main road.

"But I need more!" Willis protested.

"Not after icing your employer." The guy in the leather pants gestured at a box Willis held. "That thing's twice as hot now."

"It can't be traced."

"Like hell it can't. Fifty thousand or nothing."

Willis slumped, clicking his tongue. "Fine."

He handed over the box. The man in leather reached inside his jacket and pulled out an envelope. Willis took it and turned back toward his car.

Remi and Daniel leapt out.

"FBI! Get down on the ground with your hands behind your head!"

Willis froze, staring. The man in leathers reached inside his jacket. Remi turned to aim at him but he was already drawing.

Daniel fired first, hitting him in the lower abdomen. The man doubled over, letting out a grunt and dropping his gun. Remi turned her gun back to point at Willis.

He hadn't moved a muscle.

"Drop the envelope and get face down on the ground with your hands behind your head," she ordered.

He did as he was told, shaking all over.

Remi spared a glance in Daniel's direction. He had kicked the suspect's gun away and was cuffing the man in leathers. Detective Foster was already on the phone, calling an ambulance.

Remi hurried over and cuffed Willis, who lay on the ground shivering.

"Donald Willis, I am arresting you on suspicion of theft, trafficking in stolen goods, and the murder of Michael Grayson."

* * *

An hour later, Willis sat in a interrogation room at the local police station, looking utterly defeated. The fence's bullet wound, while painful and leading to a serious loss of blood, was not life threatening and he was now under guard and being prepped for surgery.

Sitting on the table in the interrogation room was the little box Willis had exchanged for an envelope containing $50,000 in cash. The box contained a Rolex.

That was why they hadn't found any missing antiquities. Willis hadn't stolen any. They had been so focused on Grayson's fabulous collection they hadn't even checked his personal items.

Willis had waived his right to having an attorney present and, as Remi, Daniel, and the detective faced him, told his story.

"I came into the house around eight that morning. I wanted to get everything done early that day because I was going to go into D.C. in the afternoon and have some time off. The minute I got there I knew something had gone wrong. Valentina's coat wasn't hanging in the staff room and the kitchen didn't look like it had been used to make breakfast. And she always leaves a pot of coffee hot and ready for everyone else when they get in. But the coffee had boiled over and made a big mess. The whole place stank of burnt coffee. Someone had turned the stove off but hadn't bothered to clean up. That wasn't like her at all.

"When I started walking around the house, I noticed almost no lights on, another unusual thing, and then I came to the first display room. You saw how they were.

"My first thought was that burglars had come in and tied them up. I ran back to the kitchen and grabbed a knife, then searched the house. I didn't need to search long."

Willis let out a little shudder. Remi studied him, wondering if it was genuine.

"When I saw they were dead, I panicked. At first I thought maybe I'd be a suspect. Mr. Witherspoon, the butler and head of staff, has always had it in for me, the stuffy old limey. Thinks he's in a real-life *Downton Abbey*. Anyway, I just stood there for a moment, not knowing what to do.

"Then I figured, whatever happened I was going to lose my job, and I was probably going to get suspected of the murder, so I might as well get something I could sell to have money to get down to Mexico. Been down there a lot and I speak some Spanish. I can handle myself south of the border. Plus I knew this guy who fenced stolen goods. I … well, I guess you'll find this out sooner or later … I've stolen from employers before. But I've never hurt anyone. Valentina was cool with me, and Grayson paid me well. I'd never kill anyone. You got to believe me!"

Remi studied him for a moment longer.

No, I don't think you would. The way you stole one of the least valuable things in the house, the way you cowered in the gunfight, the way you've confessed everything without even asking for a lawyer. You're a small man caught up in big affairs, Mr. Willis, and I don't think you're capable of a double homicide.

Which means the real killer is still out there somewhere.

She looked over at Daniel and Detective Foster, and saw they felt the same.

Detective Foster asked, "Can anyone vouch for your whereabouts the night your boss was killed."

"No," the prisoner said. His eyes lit up a moment later. "Wait, yes! I was at Rogan's Rowhouse that night. Stayed until about two in the morning. Ask them. Hey, you don't even need to. He's got a security camera."

"We'll check on it," the detective said.

"Where's this bar?" Daniel asked.

"Down the highway," Detective Foster said. "A good hour's drive from the scene of the crime."

Damn. That puts him well away from the scene of the crime just around when it was occurring. Time to get back to work. The only problem is, we have no real leads.

And the longer we take to find some, the harder it will be to catch up with the murderer.

CHAPTER EIGHT

Two down, two to go.

Grayson had died well, refusing to the last to reveal the item's location. Protecting his treasure like a true collector should. He couldn't fault him for that, but he couldn't let him live either. For Grayson, the piece was nothing but an ancient curio, another interesting bit to be added to a collection that spans all of human history.

What blindness. It was so much more than that.

And in his hands he would make it into something wondrous.

At least once he got all the pieces. That was going to take time, and care. You don't kill someone like Michael Grayson and not launch a massive police investigation.

The system always protected the rich and let the little people down.

If Grayson had gotten cancer, he could have afforded the best medical care, an expert team of medical personnel. Regular people? They got second-rate care that only prolonged the agony.

"The bastard deserved to die," he growled.

"¿Que?"

The taxi driver looked at him curiously in the rearview mirror. He had spoken out loud again? A bad habit. He had to keep that under control.

"Nada, chaval. Lo siento," he replied.

The taxi driver turned back to watch the road, probably thinking he had yet another drunk tourist in his back seat.

They sped along a brilliant, sun-soaked coastline. To his right rose rugged mountains, a mottling of tan rock and the deep green of bushes and trees. Here and there, dotting the slopes, stood stone huts of shepherds and a few clusters of sheep looking like little clouds in the distance. To his left spread the sea, glittering in the sun. A beach spread out alongside, where families lounged on the sand or strolled in the shallows as children laughed and splashed and chased each other.

A happy scene, one that should make him smile. But he couldn't smile, hadn't smiled in so long.

That would change. Once he got every piece, it would all change.

"Estamos aqui," the *taxista* said as he pulled into a small village square. A church, its ornate façade seeming out of place in a village of a few hundred simple homes with whitewashed walls and roofs of red tile, stood to one side. An imposing stone municipal building stood on the other. Kids on bikes circled an old monument at the center of the plaza while pensioners sat on benches, the men in black caps, the women in dresses that hadn't been fashionable for decades. Some of the women wore all black, showing they were widows. He pitied them. He knew a thing or two about mourning.

He paid and got out. The sun beat down on him but that didn't matter. He was accustomed to working outside in hot conditions. He walked with a long, quick stride out of the plaza and along a side street that sloped downhill and quickly left the village, hugging the coastline.

Soon he came to open countryside, the fields broken here and there by large haciendas of the wealthy. This part of the coastline was one of the few that hadn't been spoiled by tourism. Most of those families frolicking on the beach were locals, or tourists from another part of the country. The hacienda owners had resisted the temptation to sell their property to hotel developers or rent out rooms through Airbnb and kept the places for themselves.

"Good for them," he muttered. "Preserve what joy you have. It's so fleeting."

There he goes talking out loud again. He needed to watch that. He'd gotten fired for doing that. Not that he could focus on work after …

He staggered, stopping on the shoulder of the road and burying his face in his hands.

God, he hated this. Sometimes grief simply overwhelmed him. He had been so happy, and now this.

"You OK, mister?"

He flinched, startled. Wiping his eyes, he saw a twelve-year-old boy on a bike not far in front of him. He had been so absorbed in his own thoughts he hadn't even seen the kid approach.

The boy had one foot down on the pavement, the other still on the peddle. Long tanned limbs in red shorts and a bright green soccer jersey from some team he couldn't identify. An innocent face under straight black hair brushed neatly across the forehead. Brown eyes looked at him with open concern.

A good kid, to stop his ride to the beach or some friend's house to ask a weeping foreigner if he was OK.

The kind of kid we could have had.

That almost overwhelmed him again. He wiped his eyes a second time and put on a smile.

"I'm OK. Thank you for asking."

"You sure? You no seek?"

Sick, he almost corrected, the old teacher in him wanting to come out.

"Just a bit sad. You see, I lost someone."

The boy looked around.

Now he smiled for real. "I didn't mean lose that way. Someone I loved died."

The boy's face fell. "I lose my *abuela* this year."

Feeling bad for making a cloud pass over this boy's sunny day, he changed the subject.

"You speak very good English."

The boy immediately brightened.

Amazing how children can go from sad to happy in barely a second. I guess I could, once upon a time.

"I get a *sobresaliente* in English. My teacher he says I am the best in class."

"Your teacher is right. I bet you're good at all your other subjects too."

The boy crinkled his little nose. "No maths. Is boring."

The man laughed. "I always found math boring too. It's useful, though."

The boy shifted in his seat, looking down the road, his young mind no doubt casting ahead to whatever exciting adventure he had been bicycling towards when he met this foreigner on the road.

He suddenly felt a terrible loneliness. He wanted to prolong the conversation, take the kid for a coke at one of the village cafes, or even go to the beach with him. Anything for some company.

But of course he couldn't. That would be misunderstood, here just as much as in the United States. He didn't want the boy to think he was a bad person, because he wasn't.

He *wasn't*. He had reasons for his actions.

"You better get going," he forced himself to say. "You off to the beach?"

A grin. "Yes. Me and Mario will swim."

"Sounds like fun."

The boy looked concerned again. "You sure you OK?"

He smiled and nodded. "Yes. I'm much better now, thanks to you."

"OK. Have fun today. Go to the beach. Is great!"

The boy started to peddle and shot by him with a blur of brown limbs.

He turned to watch as the kid picked up speed, heading for the village and its trails down to the beach.

When the boy got about a hundred yards away, he turned, flashed a grin again, and waved.

"Look!" he shouted, then popped a wheelie.

"Bravo!" the man shouted, clapping.

He watched the boy until he pedaled out of sight.

Once he was gone, the smile slowly faded from the man's face. He turned back toward his destination, and trudged purposely onwards.

There was a villa not far from here, a villa owned by another collector, another man who had a part of what he needed. Another selfish rich man hoarding for himself what could help so, so many.

He'd kill that man.

CHAPTER NINE

Remi rubbed her eyes with fatigue. She had been sitting in Grayson's office for hours, going through every item in the catalog and then checking its location in the exhibition rooms. After a couple of hours of that not yielding any results, she switched to a new tactic—she started checking another ledger that listed the items not on display.

Like with museums, large private collections generally had a lot more in storage than they did on exhibition. Everyone wanted to show off their best pieces, and Grayson was no exception, even though he had filled his house with rare items. Still, he had boxes in a storage room upstairs full of old coins, ceramic lamps from the Roman and Israelite periods, Anglo-Saxon brooches, and a thousand other relics from past civilizations. Many of the items in these boxes were not in perfect condition and thus not a first choice for putting on show, but had been bought to satisfy Grayson's insatiable thirst for acquisition.

This was a much longer process, aided by Grayson's immaculate filing system, something he appeared to do all by himself. Another hallmark of the dedicated collector.

Remi started with the most recent acquisition and worked her way back. From previous cases, she knew that collectors were generally killed for something acquired recently that someone else wanted, so that seemed the best search method.

Still, it took time, crosschecking that each Athenian coin, each Neolithic clay figurine, was in its place. The listings each had a photograph attached, so she could make sure that not only was the item in its place, but that it hadn't been exchanged for something else. A time-consuming and meticulous task. That was all right. Remi was used to long hours of intense concentration.

Then, several hours into her search while Daniel did background research on Grayson and his contacts in another room, she hit on it.

She found an item that was missing. One of the boxes that contained several items of bronze of various periods from Greece, had a missing piece.

Staring at the photograph in the index, however, she had no idea what this thing was.

It looked like a piece of a machine. Or pieces.

It consisted of three parts, connected by bolts that went through holes in the ends of each piece. They looked like they were intended to move.

One piece was straight, with a hole on the far end connected to nothing. The second, middle piece was connected to the other end of this piece and was shaped a bit like a seahorse. At the end it was connected to a hexagon that had holes on each corner, one of which was connected to the seahorse. Regular lines along the circumference of the hexagon looked like they were meant to measure something.

The label said only, "Portion of mechanical device. Function unknown. C. 1st or 2nd century BC."

She stared at it for a while, trying to figure out what it could be. In the end she had to agree with Grayson's assessment—"function unknown."

It reminded her a bit of the Antikythera mechanism, a surprising find from a Greek shipwreck dating to roughly the same period.

The Antikythera mechanism was discovered back in 1901. When found, it looked like a corroded lump of bronze encased in a nearly disintegrated wooden box. Soon investigators noticed a large gear barely visible through the corrosion on one side. This caused much consternation. The ancient Greeks had gears?

Even more surprises came when the thing was x-rayed. The images showed that the artifact was actually several interlocking gears.

Archaeologists were baffled. The thing looked for all the world like the mechanism for a grandfather clock, a device totally out of place in the ancient world. Some even theorized it was a more modern machine that fell off a boat and just happened to land in the middle of a Greek shipwreck. Archaeologists could get quite creative when faced with things they didn't understand.

For years, the Antikythera mechanism, as it was dubbed, sat in the museum in Athens, a baffling curio and object of much speculation by hacks who pointed to it as proof of Atlantis or alien astronauts. It was only in modern times that better imaging technology was able to see more clearly inside the device, peering through the corrosion that had fused the parts together.

It was found to have 37 gears and various other parts. X-ray tomography revealed markings on the gears, as well as Greek writing. After long study, researchers worked out that this was actually an analogue computer that could predict eclipses, mark the motions of the Moon and other heavenly bodies, and even keep track of in which city a series of games, similar to the Olympics, would be held every four years.

Remi remembered reading about the Antikythera mechanism when she was a child and thrilling to the fact that the ancient Greeks had been so technologically advanced. That idea was much more intriguing than Martians coming down to Earth, giving the Greeks a computer, and then flying off to the Red Planet and leaving the poor Greeks sink in a storm.

So was this object from the Grayson collection part of something similar? While she didn't see any writing, that didn't mean there wasn't any. Writing was only discovered on the Antikythera mechanism with the use of advanced imagery. A simple photograph wouldn't show it under all the corrosion.

But what was clear was that it was part of a larger device. While this one part would be worth little on the illegal antiquities market, together with all the other pieces, the complete device would be priceless.

Which meant their killer either had or felt confident that he could get all the other pieces, and that would make leaving behind all the other artworks in the Grayson mansion worth it.

And that brought up a new and terrible possibility.

The thief wasn't done killing to get what he wanted.

Remi blinked. Wait, she had heard of this thing before. Some chance remark at a conference a few years ago. Mike Collins, an archaeologist at UCLA. He'd said something about it. What had he said?

She cast her mind back, closing her eyes to help her concentration.

Yes, he had mentioned a device found in an excavation in the Peloponnese, the southern peninsula of the Greek mainland and home to a host of ancient sites, not the least of which were Mycenae, Corinth, and Olympia. He had shown her a photograph and it had looked similar, cracking the joke, "Looks like the cryptex has a rival!"

Could this be the same thing? If so, it was another of Grayson's illegal acquisitions. Anything uncovered in a modern excavation had to go to the local or national museum.

Remi used her phone to take a photo of the image of the strange three interlocking pieces, sent it to Collins, and then called him. She had no time to waste.

"Hello?" the man's familiar voice came through the phone.

"Mike, this is Remi. I just sent you a photo. Was this the device you mentioned being found in the Peloponnese a few years ago?"

Mike laughed. "Same old Remi! We haven't talked in a year and you dive straight into an academic question."

"Oh, sorry. How's Rebecca? And Jim?"

"Rebecca's just fine. Jim just turned five."

"Five? My my, where does the time go?"

A strange tugging came to her heart at the mention of Mike's child. She had had no time for children, hadn't really thought about it until recently, but now she was reaching an age where she needed to make a decision about that, and the feeling was only growing.

"Hold on, let me look," Mike said. "Oh yes, this is the device. Well, part of it. The mechanism was broken when found and there were four parts, each with several components. It all must fit together somehow but no one knows how. There might be some parts missing. Archaeologists hardly ever find all the pieces of anything. One of the more annoying aspects of my job. Why are you asking about this?"

"This was stolen."

"I know."

Remi blinked. "What? How do you know?"

"It was stolen along with some other artifacts from the storage area of the archaeological site during the field season. They never even got a chance to move it to the regional museum or even begin with its restoration. That's why so little is known about it. Terrible loss."

"When was this?"

"Five years ago. Wait, I'm confused. If you knew it was stolen, why are you asking?"

"Because the piece I sent you a photograph of was stolen again. It was bought illegally by a rich collector named Michael Grayson and he was killed for it."

"Killed for it? So why are you … wait. You really are working for the FBI? Sandy told me that but I thought she was joking."

Remi smiled. "Sometimes it doesn't seem real to me either."

"Wow. Time really does fly. But what about your academic career?"

Remi felt another tug at her heart. "I've … taken a leave of absence."

She couldn't quite bring herself to admit that this leave of absence would in all likelihood last a lifetime.

"Oh, I see. Well, that's good. We wouldn't want to lose you. I like how you rile things up. Get all the old stuffy scholars upset with your theories. You always liked a good fight."

"Some more than others," Remi replied, thinking of the gunfight at the abandoned gas station. "So no one knows where the pieces disappeared to?"

"No. But I heard a rumor that a guy in England uncovered one on the black market. What was his name? Oh, right. Carstairs Brentford. Independent scholar. One of these rich guys living off an inheritance who decides to be an academic. Someone who visited him told me he saw one of the parts in Brentford's collection. I informed the London police and they checked but didn't find it. Brentford said his visitor must have been mistaken. My guess is that he saw my colleague notice the piece and he moved it to a safety deposit box or something."

"Thank you so much, Mike. If you think of anything else, let me know."

"Will do."

Remi got on her computer and looked up Carstairs Brentford. He had a basic website that linked to some of his articles in various minor journals and newsletters. There was no contact information except for an email address. Remi needed something a bit faster than that. A quick search found his home telephone number in London. She rang it. It was evening in England, but not too late.

A woman with a working class English accent answered.

"Hello. Brentford residence."

"Hello. May I speak to Carstairs Brentford, please?"

Pause. When the woman spoke again, her voice wavered. "I'm sorry, haven't you heard?"

"Heard what?" Remi asked, with a sinking feeling that she knew.

That got confirmed a moment later.

"Mr. Brentford was the victim of a break-in a week ago. He's been murdered. I'm his cleaner. The police only allowed me in today after clearing the crime scene. They left it such a mess. I'm supposed to clean up before his daughter puts the house up for sale."

Remi took a deep breath. "My name is Remi Laurent, special agent with the American FBI."

"Oh, I see." The woman sounded confused, no doubt wondering why someone with a French accent would identify themselves as an FBI agent.

"Do you know the name of the investigating officer?"

"Yes. Oh, one minute. He gave me his card. Such a nice Asian gentleman. Very sympathetic."

After a moment, and some sounds of the cleaner rummaging through her purse, the woman said, "Oh, here it is. Detective Chief Inspector Arjun Gupta. I'll give you his email and mobile number."

"Thank you," Remi said, writing down the information as the woman gave it to her. When she was done, the woman asked,

"If you don't mind my asking, why is the FBI involved in this? Has there been another murder in America?"

"Yes, there has. Of a collector much like your employer."

"Gracious me. What's this world coming to?"

"I honestly don't know. Thank you for your help."

Remi hung up, then ran to where Daniel was working.

"We need to go to London!"

Daniel looked up from his computer. "We don't get our two for one yet."

"The stolen artifact was only one of four pieces of a larger device. The three other pieces went missing but a collector in London is said to have had one. Someone murdered him last week, before Grayson got killed. Why didn't the assistant director tell us?"

Daniel stood. "The British police probably didn't inform any of the international law enforcement groups, assuming it was a domestic crime. Give me all the details and let's call the Metropolitan Police. It looks like I'll need to talk the FBI into granting some travel funds."

"Right." Remi started to dial Detective Chief Inspector Gupta's number.

Daniel gave her a playful punch on the shoulder. "You sure are turning out to be handy."

Remi flushed, enjoying the approval and, she had to admit, the way Daniel looked at her. She dialed the number, heart racing fast. They were off on another hunt.

CHAPTER TEN

Remi yawned as they passed through the arrival gate at Heathrow, Daniel at her side. A middle-aged Indian man in a conservative suit, hair trimmed short and with a bit of a belly, stood holding a sign with their names on it.

Remi walked over to him. "Detective Chief Inspector Arjun Gupta? I'm Trainee Agent Remi Laurent and this is Special Agent Daniel Walker."

"Pleased to meet you," Gupta said, shaking both of their hands. "I hope you're not too tired. I think it's best if we went straight to the scene of the murder. Thank you for sending the information on the Grayson case. I agree with your assessment. It looks like we have an international killer on our hands."

They walked straight out of the terminal to a waiting car. As they climbed in, Detective Chief Inspector Gupta handed them a file.

"A print out of everything we know so far. The only person who had keys other than Carstairs Brentford was Cassie Symons, the cleaner. We checked on her and I was 99 percent certain she was innocent. Now that I've read your report of the Grayson murder I'm one hundred percent. There's also Melissa Patterson, a graduate student at the Oriental Institute who comes in part time to help with his work. She doesn't have a key to the house but either Brentford or Symons would have let her in. That doesn't matter. She was in Majorca at the time of the murder so we eliminated her as a suspect first thing."

Remi handed over a file of her own.

"This is the information Greek police gave us on the original theft five years ago. Not much to say, I'm afraid. The four pieces and a few other artifacts were stolen from a storage shed on the dig site. Common enough, I'm afraid. None of the artifacts have ever been located."

"Were the archaeological crew members investigated?" Gupta asked.

"The police searched their dormitory and the entire camp and found nothing. Their bags were searched again when they left the country. Nothing."

While Remi was a historian and not an archaeologist, their fields of study overlapped and she knew many archaeologists. An archaeological field crew was led by a dig director, the professor who organized the excavation and would publish the results. Beneath him were area supervisors, generally graduate students with excavation experience. The grunt work was done by volunteer undergraduate students and occasionally a retiree or two doing the dig on a lark.

None of these people would go through background checks, making it possible that an antiquities thief could infiltrate a dig crew. She had never heard of that happening, though. The undergraduates would be too young to know where to sell ancient artifacts, the graduate students tended to be wide-eyed idealists, and the dig director wouldn't want to risk a career carefully built up over decades.

Especially not this find. It would have made the dig director's career, given him international fame. Restoring and publishing the mechanism would have been a far bigger reward than selling it on the black market.

They drove out onto a highway and headed for central London. It was a Saturday morning and the traffic was mostly headed out of the city, so they made good time.

"So there was no sign of forced entry?" Remi asked.

"None. The cleaner and graduate student both said he was very friendly, though, and that anyone who had even the slightest reason to visit would have been allowed in. Apparently he was a rather lonely old duffer who wanted the company. We found that only one piece out of his collection was missing. The thief obviously came only for that. he or she didn't even touch the two hundred pounds in Brentford's billfold."

"Have you checked his email?" Daniel asked.

"Yes. Nothing. He mostly spoke by phone, although his phone records haven't given us any leads either. He didn't speak to anyone different in the days before the murder, just friends and known associates. We ran a check on all of them and none have flown to America in the past few days."

"So our suspect must be someone who was known to him and who just showed up, or some stranger who managed to talk his way into the house," Remi said.

"It looks like it, yes," Gupta replied.

"I've been wondering about that with the Grayson murder," Daniel said. "While he didn't have security cameras, he did have a burglar alarm that would notify a local security company if it went off. It never did. So either the killer hacked the alarm or knew the code, or Grayson let him in. But phone and email records don't show him talking to anyone we haven't checked out."

"Both men were collectors," Gupta said. "They would have known many people in the community. It's a tight-knit group. Perhaps this is another collector who is desperate to get all the pieces to this device."

Remi and Daniel nodded, then started flipping through the file. It showed a scene similar to the one at the Grayson mansion. An old man dead on the floor with severe head trauma, a note saying it was most likely done with a hammer just like the Grayson murder. The interior of a nice home that had been ransacked. This one, however, hadn't been as thoroughly torn apart as the Grayson residence. The collection here looked smaller, and the house itself, while showing prosperity, wasn't as huge as the killer's other hit. He didn't have to look as long to get what he wanted.

Then Remi came to the last page, which was a color photocopy of a page from a ledger. At the top of a page was a photograph of a large bronze plate with several holes and dowels on one side. A single gear was attached to one of these dowels. Another photo showed the back, which was flat and blank. The piece looked less corroded than the Grayson piece, as if it had been restored by a careful hand. She could see no markings or writing.

Remi and Daniel looked at each other.

"Well, there's your next piece," Daniel said. "I hope this isn't like our other thing, where we hop from one clue to the next and all we find is more mysteries."

Remi chuckled. It did seem that the cryptex was leading them on a merry chase all around the world with no end in sight.

She wondered about that. Why had the designers of the cryptex left such a baffling and far-flung trail of clues? Perhaps they figured that only the most dedicated would make the journey. It was hard enough with modern air travel, and in the days of steam engines and sailing ships it would have been well-nigh impossible. That would have stopped many people.

She also wondered about that strange medallion she had discovered in the catacombs. Remi still hadn't figured out its markings and had little time to study the issue.

Remi shook off those thoughts and focused on the matter at hand. Gupta's suggestion of a collector known to both victims made sense. It had to be someone known enough and trusted enough to be allowed into the home at night when the victims were alone.

Known and trusted? The bar for that wasn't very high. Collectors were an obsessive and rather eccentric lot, and if a dealer or fellow collector showed up with some story about a great find they'd be willing to part with, they'd be invited in with open arms. Both men had lived lives of privilege, and would not expect a seemingly friendly visitor who shared their enthusiasms to bludgeon them to death with a hammer.

"We need to crosscheck the two victims address books, phone records, and email accounts for any overlap in contacts," Remi said.

"Now you're acting like an FBI agent," Daniel said with ironic approval.

"Don't I usually?"

"No. You usually act like a bulldog."

"I will assume that's a compliment and not an insult," Remi sniffed.

They passed through central London, a city Remi had always much admired for its museums and art galleries, its mixture of sleek glass high-rises and Victorian elegance, and always disliked visiting for its pollution, smell of unhealthy food, noisy drunken crowds, and general uncleanliness. She preferred Paris. While it got subjected to a year-round tourist invasion just like London, it was far more beautiful and had decent food.

Detective Chief Inspector Gupta parked outside a Victorian brick home on a quiet side street in Mayfair, one of the more expensive boroughs in central London. The house was one of a row of houses that looked to have been built all at the same time around the turn of the last century. If Brentford owned the whole house, he had been a rich man indeed.

“I’ve asked the cleaning lady and graduate student to be here,” Gupta said as they got out. “Since you have the advantage of seeing both crime scenes, perhaps you can think of something to ask them that I haven’t.”

They walked up a flight of steps to a door with a brass knocker. Gupta rapped on this three times and within a few moments the door opened to reveal a short, plump older Englishwoman wearing a kerchief on her head.

“Oh, Melissa!” she called out to someone behind her. “The police are here already.”

They stepped into the front hallway. Old prints lined the walls, and a rather threadbare carpet covered the floor.

“I’m Cassie Symons,” she said as she shook Remi’s hand. “I believe we spoke on the telephone. Oh, here’s Melissa. Melissa Patterson, Mr. Brentford’s assistant.”

A rather prim looking young woman in her early twenties came to the front hall. She was dressed in a conservative gray sweater and matching slacks and had her hair pulled back in a bun. It made her look ten years older. She studied the officers with ill-concealed hostility from behind a pair of cat’s-eye glasses.

“Come in, come in,” Symons said. “Oh, please wipe your feet. The estate agent will be coming to look at the house to put it up for sale. The sitting room is just to the left. I think I hear the kettle. I’ll just be a moment.”

Symons hurried off to the kitchen, just visible through a half-open door at the end of the hall. The rest of them went through an open doorway to the left and into a large sitting room and library.

Floor-to-ceiling bookshelves held hundreds of volumes on Classical history, literature, and archaeology. Remi noted books in English, Latin, both ancient and modern Greek, and German. There were very few books on any other subject beyond the Classical world.

Cocooned within the fortress of books stood a sofa, three armchairs, and a few side tables. All of them looked at least a hundred years old and in need of reupholstering. The Oriental rug was in a similar state. Remi guessed that Carstairs Brentford was what the English referred to as “shabby genteel,” a man of generational wealth who lived off the interest from family investments, seeing less and less returns as inflation slowly overcame his fortune. Mike Collins had mentioned something along those lines.

Melissa sat, crossed her legs, and put her hands on her lap, fingers interlaced.

"I've already answered the inspector's questions. I fail to see the purpose of this meeting."

Her accent was posh, and indicated a young woman who had enjoyed all the good things of life. Remi had encountered many of her French counterparts at the Sorbonne. They seemed to be able to sniff out her middle-class origins and judge her for it. She suspected Melissa had gotten a whiff too.

Remi walked over and stood close in front of her, a technique of intimidation she had learned in her training just a couple of weeks before.

"So you were in charge of researching and documenting Carstairs Brentford's collection?"

"I do believe I mentioned that previously."

"Not to me you haven't." Remi found herself imitating Daniel's gruff manner, something that had always annoyed her, although she had to admit it yielded results.

"What can you tell me about the missing piece?"

"Very little. He acquired it several months ago. He—"

"From whom?"

"He didn't tell me. He was quite private about his financial affairs," Melissa replied, looking annoyed at the interruption.

"Go on."

"The piece looks Ancient Greek, dating to just before the Roman conquest in the second century B.C.. It appears to be part of a larger device similar to the Antikythera mechanism. That's a—"

"I'm familiar with the Antikythera mechanism."

"Yes, I suppose you looked it up on Wikipedia."

This young woman was not helping Remi's national distaste for the English.

Before she could think of a cutting response, Cassie Symons returned with a large tray with a teapot, china cups, and a plate of bland-looking biscuits.

"Show us the collection, and also the notes you kept for Mr. Brentford," Remi said.

The older woman put the tea tray down and started pouring.

Melissa turned to the cleaning lady. "I *am* sorry, Mrs. Symons, but I think your efforts have been wasted. They want to nose around the collection."

Remi seriously doubted Melissa had ever apologized to the cleaning lady for anything ever before.

The graduate student got up with a put-upon expression and led them to a back room as spacious as the front. Large windows overlooked a sizeable back garden with a lawn, several trees with leaves turning autumn colors, and a flowerbed. Few people had a garden this large in London, or indeed a garden at all.

But what captivated Remi's immediate attention were the antiquities all around her.

Several bas-reliefs of gods and goddess, which had no doubt once adorned ancient temples, hung on the walls. In each corner stood a small Greek or Roman statue, each in a good state of preservation. A framed collection of carved Roman intaglios were all of the highest quality, and there was even a papyrus written in Greek from the time of the Ptolemaic dynasty. In the middle of the room stood a long display case filled with gold coins and a few Greek plates with painted scenes of warriors, satyrs, and dryads. While not as extensive as the Grayson collection, it showed care and the finest of taste. Remi found herself wishing she could have met the man behind it.

"Where was the piece that was stolen?" Remi asked.

"Box 54," Melissa said. "As I told the Detective Chief Inspector."

She pulled out a long box from a shelf of similar boxes and opened it. Inside were mounted several pieces of ancient Greek bronze, including figurines and brooches, all labeled with an accession number. An empty space with the device's accession number was right in the center.

Remi looked around. Besides the shelves of boxes, she saw a desk, a computer, and a stack of academic journals. Most people subscribed to the digital editions these days, but it appeared that the elderly Brentford preferred hard copy.

She moved over, intending on looking at the journals, then got stopped by something else.

A small, leather-bound diary poking out from the bottom of the pile.

"What's this?" Remi asked, reaching for it.

Melissa snatched it before she could.

"It's Mr. Brentford's personal diary! There's no need to pry into his personal affairs."

Remi, Daniel, and Detective Chief Inspector Gupta all stared at each other for a moment in reaction to this ridiculous statement, and then as one reached their hands out for it.

Melissa burst out in tears. Remi took half a step back in surprise. It was like seeing a glacier suddenly melt before your eyes. The graduate student clutched the diary to her chest. Remi stepped forward and gently pried it out of her grasp.

Looks like we found what we came for, she thought as she hefted the thick little volume. *I wonder what this is going to tell us?*

CHAPTER ELEVEN

Remi tried to ignore Daniel's eating habits while studying the diary. Her partner had checked them into a hotel in an old building well past its prime, with dirty carpet and suspicious-smelling bathrooms. The appeal, at least for Daniel, was that it was situated above a pub, where hotel residents got a discount. Daniel was tucking into fish and chips and a pint of ale. Remi had ducked out to the nearest supermarket and grabbed some fruit and crackers. She'd eat in her room.

"This diary shows why Melissa has such a bad attitude," Remi said, having to raise her voice over the loud conversation of the crowd of English drinkers.

"What have you found?" Daniel asked around a mouthful of cod that had probably been frozen for the past decade and put through a microwave in the pub's "kitchen."

"Melissa had feelings for him, or at least pretended to. Listen to this, it's from a month ago:

"Melissa is still acting the amusing distraction. Every time she reaches over to point out something while I'm seated at my desk, she manages to press her chest against my shoulder. And just this morning she asked to wash up in the bathroom. She took her shirt off to wash her hands and face and didn't even close the door all the way! I would be scandalized if I wasn't so tickled.

"I suppose I should feel flattered. She's after my money, though. She's too young to realize that at my age, a man of my wealth has seen this thing far too many times before. What I won't tell her is that she's in my will. Enough to pay off any student loans she might have. It won't change her life in any fundamental way, but it will help her along to the next step of life.

"Perhaps I should tell her, although that might just encourage her. What she doesn't understand is that even if I was young enough to care about such things, I still wouldn't. I thought young people were a bit more savvy about this sort of thing. Ah well, at least she doesn't know about J. If she suspected the existence of that little minx, it would drive her mad!"

"Well, that's interesting," Daniel said. "And how much do you want to bet our little graduate student read that?"

"I'm sure she did. Do you think she did it?"

"Jealousy over this mysterious J? Perhaps. But she's in the will, and if it's money she's after, I doubt she'd kill him right off. She seems too smart for that. No, I think she'd work on him, talk about those student loans and maybe invent a sick uncle or two. Killing him would guarantee that she'd get only what's in the will and nothing more."

"Perhaps she has financial difficulties."

"Gupta said Brentford paid her well and that she came from a rich family. He checked on the cleaning lady too. Neither had any emergencies that would require them to murder and steal from his collection. Want some of this?"

He held out a forkful of unappealing fried fish.

"How can you eat that?" Remi asked.

Daniel shrugged. "It's popular here. When in Rome, eat as the Romans do."

"If we were in Rome, we'd be eating real food."

"This is real food."

"I wonder who J. is?" Remi said, turning back to the diary. "And why didn't Melissa hide the diary? It doesn't put her in a very good light."

"Maybe she was afraid to tamper with a crime scene. Maybe she was so flustered by the murder she forgot. People act unpredictably in situations like this. Whatever the reason, it actually puts her in a favorable light. If she had bumped him off, she'd have burned the thing."

"Good point," Remi said, nodding. "I've noticed that every three or four days the date has an exclamation point behind it."

"Maybe a visit by this J. person?"

"Perhaps. I'm not finding any more references to J., though. And nothing regarding acquiring the device."

"Keep looking. That's a pretty thick journal. It might be in there somewhere."

"Yes," Remi grumbled. "I have a long night of reading ahead."

"Like every other night in your life," Daniel said with a smile.

“No, sometimes I stare at this.” Remi took out the medallion she had found in the catacombs.

Daniel’s eyebrows shot up. “You brought that along?”

“Of course. I didn’t dare leave it in my house. Someone might break in and search for it.”

“True enough. You’ve picked up some enemies I guess I have too. Thanks for that.”

“Sorry.”

“That’s OK. Keeps me on my toes.”

Remi looked at the medallion again. “I’m just hoping if I look at it enough, the answer will come to me.”

Daniel grinned. “And if you weren’t on a case you’d be staring at it all day and night.”

“You know me well,” Remi smiled, then grew serious. “Something has been worrying me. Whatever happened to the Order of St. Adrian of Nicomedia?”

This was an ancient order that was sworn to protect the cryptex and its secrets.

Daniel snapped his fingers. “Hey, you’re right. We haven’t come across them since the Cryptex Killer case. They must know you’re on the trail. So why have they been so silent?”

Remi shrugged. “I have no idea. It worries me.”

“Maybe they got warned off by the Society of Devout Students?”

“They’ve been around so long I have a hard time believing they could be warned off unless … unless they got warned off by the Vatican Police.”

Daniel winced. “That could make things pretty dicey.”

“I’m sorry I dragged you into this.”

Daniel smiled and gave her a sidelong look. “Are you?”

“I don’t want you to get in trouble.”

“I came in with my eyes open.”

Remi plucked the medallion out of his hand. “I’m going to leave you to your plate of congealed grease and eat some real food in what passes for my room. I’ll try to get through the whole diary tonight.”

“All right. Try to get some sleep too. They offer a full English breakfast starting at eight.”

Remi curled her lip. Bacon. Sausage made from God-knows-what. Baked beans on toast. Revolting, especially the last part. Baked beans was something you gave to prisoners convicted of terrible crimes, not real people. And to put it on some cheap white bread so it got all mushy … it made her shudder just to think about.

Daniel's phone buzzed.

"The assistant director?" Remi asked.

Daniel looked at his phone and the corner of his mouth twitched. "No, Veronica."

Daniel and Veronica had divorced just a few months before, and now Veronica wanted to get back together. Remi didn't know what Daniel thought about that. He hadn't exactly been forthcoming about the subject. Being such a private man, getting annoyed by the strangest things, she had been afraid to ask.

From what she saw from the one time she had met Veronica, those two were poorly matched. She was certainly good looking, and judging from what Daniel said quite successful at business, but she seemed a bit cold, a bit aloof. Remi got the impression that she bossed Daniel around a bit and could be demanding. Remi couldn't imagine anyone else getting away with that.

The biggest mark against her was that Remi was almost certain that she didn't bother to understand Daniel. True, that was a hard thing to do, but it was something all couples should do. Veronica struck her as too self-absorbed to work out the deep rooted issues that were obviously troubling Remi's partner.

Daniel needed someone more like him, someone who understood and appreciated his profession and someone willing to understand him personally.

But it wasn't her place to get involved in any of that. Stepping into other people's relationship troubles was a guaranteed recipe for disaster. Best just to give him some room. She rose.

"I'm going upstairs," Remi told him.

Daniel nodded, not bothering to look up from his texting. That nettled Remi for some reason, although she knew it wasn't fair. Why should she pay attention to her when he was trying to get back with his ex-wife?

Because I'd be better for him.

Stop that! It's unprofessional and a bad idea.

Still, the thought followed her upstairs and to her room, where she found herself very much alone.

As was her habit when something troubled her, Remi buried herself in work. That suppressed the thought and the emotions behind it.

Almost.

* * *

Two hours later, eyelids heavy, Remi decided to go to sleep. She had read enough of Brentford's diary to realize she wouldn't find any easy clues. What she had found, however, was that the exclamation points behind the dates only started about four months before, and had occurred every two or three days with regularity.

The entries for these dates appeared no different than the others. The diary mostly discussed acquisitions for his collection, lectures he had attended at the Royal Society of Antiquaries, and the few social events he went to with other members of his social class. She also came across the occasional wry comment about Melissa's attempts at flirtation.

But there was nothing to indicate he had any shady dealings. Remi wondered if he had been duped into buying an illegal artifact. It seemed possible.

In that case, when whoever it had been who raised a hammer against him, the poor man had no idea why he was getting murdered.

Besides the exclamation points, Remi did notice another odd thing about the diary. Every now and then there'd be a little star on the page. Not at the top where the date was, but at some point further down. Remi puzzled over this for some time until she realized that it could correspond to the time of day. Sometimes the star was near the top, where Brentford related what he did in the morning. Sometimes it was opposite his account of the afternoon or evening. Did this mark a time of day that he had done something or gone somewhere? Whenever there was a star, the text didn't seem to cover enough activity in that time of the day to take up all the hours. That could just be coincidence—much of his day was spent simply reading—but it could be significant.

Whatever it meant, she'd have to figure it out tomorrow. Jetlag was tugging her down. She'd sleep soundly tonight.

Setting the diary on the bedside table, she switched off the lamp beside it and got comfortable. Within a minute she drifted into a heavy sleep.

In her dreams she ran through the catacombs, lit by an eerie red light. She heard sounds behind her, sounds of pursuit. She turned to warn Daniel, and found herself alone.

Alone in the catacombs. Alone with the dead. The sounds of pursuit grew louder, but it did not sound like running footsteps. Instead, it sounded like a slow creeping.

How could it be getting louder if she herself was running? And what was that sound as of someone fumbling around close to her?

The red light grew brighter. The catacombs faded.

Suddenly Remi's eyes snapped open and she sat bolt upright in bed. She wasn't dreaming. This was real!

A shadow by her bed. She let out a scream. A dim red light shone straight in her face. A hand reached for her.

Instinctively she reached for the bedside table, past where the figure stood. The shadow jumped back as if in surprise and Remi's hand grasped her small bottle of pepper spray.

"No!" a male voice whispered.

A hand reached for her wrist, grasping it just as she pressed the spray.

"Augh!" The stranger shouted as he got enveloped in a stinging cloud.

He wrenched her arm to one side and Remi ended up spraying all around her. She managed to close her eyes just in time, but in her fear and half-asleep confusion she didn't hold her breath.

Her nostrils, throat, and lungs felt like they had caught fire.

"Daniel!" she shouted, but her words only came out as a gasp.

The figure stumbled and fell hard on the floor, knocking over the lamp on the bedside table with a crash. Remi sputtered, moving away to the other side of the bed in an attempt to get away from the noxious cloud. She opened one eye, which immediately began to itch, but she didn't dare close it again.

The only light came from a bit of streetlight filtering through the curtains and the dim red flashlight the intruder had dropped.

And that intruder was rising to his feet. As Remi receded further, her sleep-muddled mind trying to recall here she had left her gun, the figure grabbed the flashlight and shone it on the bedside table.

Right on Brentford's journal.

He grabbed it, just as Remi remembered that her gun lay under her coat on the chair on this side of the room.

Trying to see through the tears forming on her one open eye, she ducked for it, tossing aside her coat and grabbing her weapon.

Just then a strong hand clamped down on her wrist.

CHAPTER TWELVE

A crash from the room next door woke Daniel up. He was out of his bed and grabbing his gun in an instant. The last fragments of a dream about Remi and Veronica were still fading from his mind as he burst out of his hotel room and ran to Remi's room next door.

A dream about his partner and his ex-wife? What was that all about?

Not important and almost immediately forgotten. Remi's door stood somewhat ajar, and he could see a wavering red light and hear the sounds of a struggle.

He tore the door open and saw Remi wrestling with a thin, short man who clutched something that Remi tried to get from him.

His trained mind made a split-second assessment. A sharp tang of pepper spray told him Remi had used her favorite weapon. The way the two fighters told him she'd gotten almost as big of a dose as the intruder had. Daniel also saw no gun, no knife, and thankfully no hammer.

Remi's gun lay on the floor near her bedside table, and the two seemed to be fighting over Brentford's diary.

Was this even their killer? Whoever he was, he was about to get his ass royally kicked.

All this passed through his mind in less than a second while running into the room. He took his finger off the trigger to avoid accidental discharge, grabbed Remi's assailant by the collar, and pulled.

He put his full weight into the movement. The stranger staggered back, and Daniel backpedaled with him, speeding up and swinging the man around so he smashed face first into the wall of the hallway. Then Daniel reversed course and slammed him into the doorjamb. The man's knees buckled and he fell to the ground with a satisfying thud.

Daniel landed on his chest, knees first, knocking the wind out of him. A left cross to the face took the last of the fight out of him. Another punch knocked him out. A third punch made Daniel feel better about getting woken up.

Remi staggered out of the room.

"You OK?" Daniel asked.

"He broke in somehow when I was asleep!" she cried.

A door down the hall opened a crack. The startled face a middle-aged man peeked out.

"What the bloody hell is going on out here?"

"Call the police," Daniel ordered.

"Excellent idea," the Englishman said. The door slammed shut again.

The light was on in the hallway, so Daniel got a good look at the assailant for the first time …

… and immediately suspected that this was not the killer.

He looked young, twenty at most, and so probably did not have the knowledge or connections to carry out antiquities thefts on two different continents.

The intruder wore fashionable clothes and had carefully managed blonde hair. His face, except for a blossoming black eye and several other fresh bruises, was strikingly handsome. If Daniel had to guess his profession he would say a male model. He certainly had the trendy clothes to match.

"Look," Remi said. She picked up a key card from the floor, pressed it against the lock in her room, and the light switched to green.

"That's not yours?" Daniel asked.

"No," Remi said, wiping her bloodshot eyes.

A thumping on the stairs. The landlord, as they called pub owners in this country, came running up.

"What's going on here?" he demanded.

"We caught an intruder," Daniel said.

"I'll call the coppers."

"One of your guests is already doing that."

The landlord, a man whose prodigious belly and ruddy face showed a fondness for his product, leaned over the unconscious man/boy.

"Oi! I know this little bugger. He was mincing around the pub half the night."

"Was he?" Daniel looked at him again. Come to think of it, he did look familiar. Daniel had a vague memory of him cadging drinks at the bar.

“He must have been spying on us and discovered our room,” Remi said. “Then he managed to get a spare key card while the landlord’s back was turned.”

“How did he find out where we were staying?” Daniel snapped his fingers. “Wait, he didn’t need to. Remember before we left we told Gupta where we were staying? We said that right in front of Cassie Symons. Melissa Patterson had just left.”

“So the cleaning lady told this man to break into my hotel room?” Remi said. Her tone of disbelief matched Daniel’s own feelings.

“That doesn’t sound right, I know. But how else to explain it?”

Remi didn’t have an answer for that, but the landlord did have some good advice.

“Um, mate, the coppers will be here pretty soon. You might want to put some trousers on.”

Daniel looked down and realized he was wearing what he usually wore to bed—an old Mets t-shirt and his underwear.

He looked at Remi with sudden terror. Remi, wearing a proper pair of pajamas, seemed to notice his state of undress only after the landlord had pointed it out. Her mouth opened in astonishment, her hand went up to cover it, and she turned a deep scarlet.

Daniel would like to have thought that was the effect of the pepper spray. Unfortunately, he knew better.

He retreated to his room, pursued by poorly stifled laughter.

Once he got decent, he had some questions for this young punk he’d pummeled.

He had some questions for the cleaning lady too.

* * *

Cassie Symons looked like she had never been to a police station in her life. Daniel tried hard not to feel sorry for her—she had endangered his partner, after all—but nevertheless he did feel some pity for the bawling woman sitting opposite them in the interrogation room.

He, Remi, and a sleepy-eyed Gupta listened as she spilled her story without any prompting.

“I am *so* sorry. I didn’t think he’d break into your room! Oh my goodness, I have really made a mess of things.”

“So how do you know Brian Edge?” Gupta said.

He was being processed as they spoke, and was already known to police. A "rent boy", as they called them here.

"Poor lad, so lost in this world," Cassie said, drying her eyes with her fifteenth Kleenex. "He was—oh, forgive me!—a sort of companion to Mr. Brentford."

"A companion?" Daniel asked, although he already knew the answer.

"Yes. You see, Mr. Brentford was, well, *musical*."

"Musical?" Daniel asked, baffled.

Gupta chuckled. "Musical is an old term for gay. I've only heard it in old movies."

Cassie Symons didn't seem the sort of person who got out much. Perhaps her view of the world had mostly come from old movies.

"Yes," Cassie said. "Although he never used that word. He was ashamed, you see. From an older generation where that sort of thing wasn't on. Now I don't want you to think those two did anything. Mr. Brentford was far too proper. He just enjoyed having him around. Sometimes I'd come to fix them dinner. Brian would even help in the kitchen, dear boy. Mr. Brentford would ask all about his acting lessons and his friends and the clubs he went to. He sort of lived through him, had the kind of life that was impossible for him when he was young."

"And he paid Brian for this," Daniel said.

"They weren't doing anything. It was company."

"What did Melissa think about him?" Daniel asked, remembering the wry comments in Brentford's journal.

"Melissa didn't know a thing about him. He only came over after she went home, and I weren't going to say anything about it not with the way she carried on. Shameful."

"And why did you tell Brian where we were staying?" Remi said.

Cassie sniffled. "I didn't thinking nothing of it. He said he thought of something that he needed to tell you, something Mr. Brentford had showed him and he thought you'd want to see it right away, so I told him where you were staying. I had no idea he'd do something like this!"

Cassie looked like she was about to burst into tears again. Remi put a hand on hers.

"It's all right. This might just help us find the person responsible for Mr. Brentford's death."

Cassie's eyes went wide. "I hope you don't think Brian did it. He wouldn't hurt a soul."

Daniel would wait and see about that. While he was ninety-nine percent sure Brian didn't wield the hammer, that didn't mean he wasn't involved somehow.

And that made him an accessory.

Daniel rose. They wouldn't get any more out of this poor woman. He, Remi, and Gupta crossed the hall to the police station's second interrogation room, a mirror image of the first.

Brian had just been placed in there. He sat ill at ease on the hard metal chair, hands clutched together between his knees, leaning slightly to the left, eyes looking up at the ceiling.

Daniel sat down hard in the chair, the steel screeching against the concrete. Brain jumped and looked at him. Remi and Gupta sat down on either side of him.

Daniel simply stared at him for a moment. He had a bandage over the cut just above the right eye, and a beautiful shiner just below. Daniel had also given him a split lip. He noticed the kid's eyes were still a bit red from the pepper spray, as were Remi's.

That pissed him off. His partner was a trainee, and it was his responsibility to protect her.

"Why did you attack an agent of the FBI?" he demanded, a bit louder than necessary. Might as well start with the big guns.

Brian didn't answer to Daniel, but to Remi.

"I didn't mean to hurt you. Honest. I just wanted Carstairs's diary."

"You two were on a first name basis, huh?" Daniel grunted.

Bria shrugged. "He was a client. My best client. All I had to do was spend time with him. Most of these old guys want more than that. With him, though, he just wanted to hear about me going out, hear about all my friends. That sort of thing. I'd scroll through my Instagram and Snapchat and tell him all about my social life. He was lonely."

Daniel detected a note of sympathy in that last statement. He decided to pounce on it.

"And now he's dead." Brian winced. Daniel leaned forward. "And a rare stolen artifact is missing from his collection. And here you come along trying to steal his diary. Why?"

"I didn't steal any artifacts from him. I don't even know anything about that stuff. He talked about it a bit, sure, but I just sort of nodded and blanked out. None of that interests me."

"Money interests you, and Brentford had a fortune."

Brain's eyes got shifty. "I'm not a killer. I had a million chances to rob the old duffer and never did."

Daniel studied him for a moment. No, he didn't think this hustler was a killer. Was he a thief? Maybe. Not while Brentford was alive. No, like Melissa he had been playing the long game, hoping to endear himself to the old man and get in the will.

When that didn't happen, he decided to take his chance.

Except he probably didn't know how to move stolen antiquities. The criminal world could be very segmented, with each specialty knowing little to nothing about the other, and Brian was only on the fringe of the criminal world. Escorts were legal in this country. This guy probably knew a dozen places to score coke, but sell an Athenian vase? Not likely.

So why the diary? Maybe Brentford mentioned some contacts in it, someone willing to buy a few items off the dead man's boytoy?

Daniel rapped his thumb against his thigh three times and leaned forward, folding his hands on the far side of the table and getting into Brian's space.

"So who is it?" he asked.

"Who is who?" Brian asked.

"The guy in the diary. The one you want to sell artifacts to."

Those bright blue eyes got shifty again. Real shifty.

Daniel raised his hand, counting off on his fingers. "Opportunity, motive, and means. You have all three, buddy. Enough to charge you with murder."

"I didn't steal anything! Check my flat."

Gupta already had, and came up with nothing except a couple of ecstasy tablets they could hold over Brian's head if he didn't start cooperating pretty soon.

"You say you didn't steal anything but I bet you know a buyer for his collection," Daniel said "You're hoping the information is in the diary."

Brian looked at his feet. For a long moment he kept silent. Daniel waited. He could tell the young man was about to crack. He didn't want to face a murder charge.

Brian took a deep breath and said, "There was this one chap, an old Spanish man who came to visit Carstairs a few months ago. Carstairs didn't know him and he came unannounced one night while he and I were alone. Cassie had already cleaned up after dinner and left us." Brian looked at them, pleading. "Please don't think Cassie has anything to do with this. She's a good sort. She never scoffed at me or put on airs like some of the client's servants."

"Go on," Daniel said.

"Carstairs usually saw his collecting chums alone. He was a bit embarrassed by me, you see, and so other than Cassie, no one knew about me, not even Melissa, the grasping cow."

Daniel waited.

"So this Spanish chap shows up. Terribly sick. Always coughing into a handkerchief. I even saw some blood on it. Other than that he could have been Carstairs's twin. Had all the same interests and started chattering away about lectures and books that I had never heard of. This Spaniard said he had some things he wanted to sell, and so Carstairs let him in."

"Does this Spaniard have a name?" Detective Chief Inspector Gupta asked.

"Sergio Ramon-Diaz."

"Did he mention where he lived?"

"Somewhere on the coast. I think he mentioned he lived close to Málaga."

Gupta got on his phone. Brian went on.

"I made them tea, and by the time I got back the conversation had changed. Turned out this fellow didn't want to sell anything at all, he wanted to buy. Wanted something he called 'your part of the device.' He explained how he was sick and he needed it. I don't know what his health had to do with anything, but Carstairs just nodded like it made sense. The Spaniard said he'd pay anything for it. He even showed Carstairs photos of his collection, telling Carstairs he could take his pick along with the money, just so he could get this one piece."

"What did Mr. Brentford say to that?" Remi asked.

"He didn't want to sell. He was very apologetic, saying he sympathized with Sergio about his illness but that two parts wouldn't be enough. The device would only work if complete."

"Did Mr. Brentford explain what he meant by that?" Daniel asked.

"No. The Spaniard seemed to understand what he meant. I was just there to serve tea. Sergio barely looked at me. Probably thought I was a grandson."

Brian chuckled at that. Daniel frowned. Brian didn't seem terribly upset at his client's death.

"What else did they say about this device?" Daniel asked..

"Nothing, at least nothing I remember. It was mostly the Spaniard badgering Carstairs to sell it to him and Carstairs politely putting him off."

"What happened next?" Daniel asked.

"Not much. The conversation went round and round, Sergio raising the price, begging even, but Carstairs wouldn't move an inch. I didn't understand what was so important about this piece. He's sold items before. Eventually Sergio left, looking like he'd lost his last hope."

"After he left, did Mr. Brentford talk about this with you?" Remi asked.

"No. He went mum. He seemed a bit down, as if turning this stranger away hurt him. He was always so kind. Never wanted to disappoint a soul. He simply told me to go, saying he was tired. He never mentioned it again."

"So why did you want the diary?"

Brian winced. "I might as well admit this to you, but I thought the diary would have information about this device. It seemed to be a puzzle Carstairs had solved. If I could get this information and the piece, I planned to sell it to Sergio."

"So you stole the piece," Daniel stated.

"No! I don't even know what it looks like. But check the diary, I'm sure it will talk about it."

"Actually it doesn't," Remi said, "but we already know what it looks like, and we know it was stolen."

Brian's eyes bugged. "It was stolen?"

"That's why Mr. Brentford was killed."

"I didn't do it. And Cassie wouldn't have done it either."

"Do you think Melissa could have done it?"

Brian thought for a moment, then shook his head. “I never met her, but from what I heard she was a manipulative little tart, but no. I don’t think she’d kill him.”

And with that, Daniel believed him. In an interrogation room faced with three officers and a murder charge, he had not implicated anyone else. That was a strong sign of innocence.

They’d hold him, of course. He was guilty of breaking and entering and attacking an officer of the law. But Daniel didn’t hold out any hopes that they had found their man.

Daniel turned to Gupta, who was still searching on his phone.

“We need to find this Spanish collector. He may be our man.”

“Or the killer’s next victim,” Gupta said.

CHAPTER THIRTEEN

Sergio Ramon-Diaz doubled over, nearly overcome with a fit of coughing. It was two in the morning, but the hour of the day or night meant little to him now. When one had such little time left to live, one didn't care about such things. Only the number of hours left mattered.

And his life could very well be counted in hours. He used to count it in months, like the doctors did, or even years.

There had been a time, not so long ago when he was still in his sixties, that he didn't count at all.

But cancer was eating his insides, spreading so quickly that no modern medicine could stop it.

They had spoken of chemotherapy and bone marrow transplants and the removal of a couple of organs. When he had asked how much more time all these procedures would give him, they merely shrugged.

"We can't say," they admitted. "A few months perhaps. Maybe a year."

Sergio decided not to be a burden on the health system. Why go through all that, suffer so much, when the end was as imminent as it was inevitable? Better to give the treatment to one of those sad little bald children he had seen on the ward. Maybe they could make it,

He certainly couldn't. Not with medicine or surgery.

Something could save him, though. If only he could get it.

Sergio wiped his mouth with his handkerchief, the green silk coming away with a few drops of blood. He shuffled out of the his bedroom, wearing a bathrobe and slippers, and into his spacious living room. There he ran a hand along the smooth marble of a statue of Diana standing next to the doorway, and ran his eyes along the bronze figurines arrayed on the side table and the fragment of Roman mosaic set under glass on the coffee table.

The old collector smiled. He was especially proud of that. When he saw that mosaic fragment up for auction, he realized the proportions were perfect for a coffee table. It made quite the conversation piece, back when he used to have visitors. Only close family and a few friends now. The rest made their excuses. He did not blame them. The smell of death did not make for an enjoyable evening.

He padded across the living room to unlock and open the sliding glass door. "Glass" was a bit of a misnomer. It was actually of the bulletproof variety. This portion of the southern Spanish coast had many wealthy homes like his, and that attracted burglars.

Another fit of coughing stopped him short. He grabbed the back of an armchair, using his other hand to cover his mouth with his handkerchief. Those spots of blood were difficult to get out of the upholstery.

He recovered after a minute, and moved over to the sliding glass doors, unlocked them, and with a grunt of effort slid them open.

The warm night breeze of the Mediterranean wafted over him. Sergio took a deep breath and stepped out on the patio. At this hour it was dark, just a few scattered lights from the other seaside villas, the rotating glow of the lighthouse a few kilometers along the shore, and the winking lights of the fishing boats far out on the water, gathering the night's catch for the early morning fish market.

Sergio moved to the railing and leaned against it with both hands to support himself. He could feel his body growing weaker with every day. A pity. Life was so sweet. So full of beauty and things of interest. It seemed unfair that someone who could appreciate it so deeply had to die a slow, painful, wasting death.

But he was resigned now. He had only one piece of the four, and of the others he had tried to trace, he had only found one. That was owned by a collector in London and he would not sell. He, too, was advanced in years, and knew what the device could do.

A soft sound on the rocky slope beside his patio caught his awareness. Sergio did not turn. Many rabbits lived along these slopes, and some of the neighborhood dogs wandered free. Such night noises did not worry him.

Until a dark figure clambered over the railing and hopped onto the patio.

Sergio gasped and took a step back.

"Who are you?" Sergio demanded. "What do you want?"

The figure stepped forward into the light from the living room. Sergio saw a man in his forties who looked in the prime of health, dressed like an Englishman or American. In one hand he gripped a hammer. The intruder shot out a beefy arm and with his free hand grabbed Sergio by the collar.

"Where is it?" he demanded in accented Spanish. Now Sergio could tell he was American.

"I-I have money. I—"

"The device. The Peloponnese mechanism. Where is it?"

Sergio took in a sharp intake of breath. "I know who you are you're—"

The shock and his ponding heart set off another burst of coughing. If the American hadn't been holding his collar, Sergio would have fallen.

"What's the matter with you?" the man asked.

Sergio kept coughing, drops of blood falling onto his bathrobe.

"Cancer? Do you have cancer?"

Sergio nodded.

The intruder's voice softened. "I knew someone who died of cancer. She coughed like you, near the end. I'm so sorry you have to suffer from this."

To Sergio's surprise, the man's sympathy sounded genuine. Ridiculous considering he had just challenged him with a hammer and had come to steal his most treasured possession.

"Come," the man said, leading him back inside.

He set Sergio in an armchair, still coughing, and closed the sliding glass door.

Sergio motioned for a decanter of water and a glass on the coffee table and the man rushed over to fill the glass for him. The care and haste with which he did this gave Sergio a spark of hope. Perhaps this man wasn't all bad after all. Perhaps he would only steal his second most treasured possession and leave him with the one thing that was still more important—his few remaining days of life.

Sergio took the glass offered him, coughed, took a sip, and his burning throat soothed. He still didn't trust himself to speak, so he merely nodded a thank you and took a couple of more sips. The man stood before him, still gripping his hammer.

"You have a nice collection," he said.

"Thank you," Sergio said. "Why … why are you here?"

The question was so desperate that Sergio almost felt ashamed. Such a weak evasion, a mock innocence that no one would believe.

Certainly not this man.

"You know why. What man in your position, knowing what you know, wouldn't try and see if it was all true?"

Sergio could only nod.

The intruder's face darkened. The shoulders slumped, the fire in the eyes guttering. But the grip on the hammer only tightened.

"You looked for it for the same reason as I am," he said.

Sergio studied him.

"You don't look sick."

The intruder only shook his head slowly, staring off far into the unseen distance.

Sergio wondered what he saw there, and felt glad not to know. It would be ugly, as ugly as Sergio's latest x-rays.

"A son? A daughter?" Sergio asked gently.

"Wife," the man said, still not focusing on Sergio.

Maybe if I sympathize he won't kill me.

What a mercenary feeling. How unworthy of your last moments.

And yet I do sympathize! So why should I die?

Run. Run while he's reminiscing.

Run for how far before he catches you? Ten meters? Five?

Just accept, Sergio. You had a good life.

If only it could have been longer.

But remember, a good one.

A sudden shudder running through the intruder's whole body snapped Sergio out of his thoughts and made him shrink back in his seat. For a second, the man before him didn't seem quite human.

The blinked twice, then turned to look at Sergio, as if remembering he was there.

"Where is it?"

Sergio waved his hand. "It is no good to you. I've searched all over for the other three pieces. No luck. They've vanished. My being able to buy the one piece I have was a stroke of good fortune. I just happened to be passing through the village in the Peloponnese when someone offered it to me. He didn't have the other pieces. Believe me, I badgered him. Offered him more money than I could afford. He didn't have them. And I never found out who else did. You won't find them either. They've vanished."

Sergio stopped talking, feeling that he had perhaps said too much, that he had acted with the feigned innocence of a child caught doing something wrong.

But he didn't want Brentford to get hurt. Sergio had raged at him for not selling him the other piece, but he could not fault him. Brentford didn't deserve a visit from this maniac.

The intruder shook his head. "I've found them."

Sergio opened his mouth to speak. The intruder cut him off.

"All of them." A trace of worry passed over the man's features, making him look human again. "I almost have them all."

Something in the way he said it made Sergio shiver.

"It's on the middle shelf in my study," Sergio said, gesturing toward the hallway, "in the gray conservation box. Take it and go. Just leave me be."

The man smiled and stepped forward, making Sergio flinch.

"Life suddenly dear? It won't be in a month or so. As I said, I've seen a case like yours before. You may feel awful now, but in a month you'll wish you felt like you do now. You'd do anything to feel that way."

The man reached down with his free hand and grabbed Sergio by the wrist. The sick old man tried to sputter out a protest, but instead struggled for breath as the intruder pulled him along down the hallway. It was all Sergio could do to stay on his feet.

The American swiped casually upward with his hammer to switch on the hallway light, and turned his head to the left and right as they passed rooms. Bathroom. Bedroom. The office, with a desk and a large rack of shelving.

The intruder pushed Sergio into the chair by the desk. He fell onto it slantwise and tumbled to the floor, instigating another fit of coughing.

With Sergio's body bent over with pain, he remained only dimly aware of the man sliding out the box from the shelf and placing it on the desk, sweeping the papers and books there off with one impatient hand. He took off the lid and tossed it aside. Sergio recovered enough to look up.

The hammer lay forgotten on the desk next to the box containing Sergio's greatest purchase. If he only had the strength to grab it, smash it into this man's knee. He didn't want to kill him, Sergio had never hurt anyone in his life. But this was self-defense. He only wanted to injure him enough that he could get away and call the police.

Sergio's coughing subsided. He edged nearer to the desk while the intruder remained distracted.

The American gasped and pulled out his fragment of the Peloponnese mechanism.

For a moment, Sergio paused, sharing his awe.

It was a circular brass plate, looking a bit like the back of an astrolabe. All around its edge with lines at regular intervals, as if to mark the progress of a clockwork or dial. At several stages were inscriptions in ancient Greek, naming parts of the body. Lungs. Eyes. Heart. In larger letters further out on the edge of the plate were the names of the four humors first identified by Hippocrates—blood, yellow bile, black bile, and phlegm. These were marked by deeper, thicker lines marking the circular plate into quadrants.

Attached to the plate were two interlocking gears, each marked by a series of numbers. Sergio had studied the significance of those numbers long and hard, even as he battled terminal cancer. After more than two years he had cracked the code. The numbers were related to ancient Greek numerology, magical numbers matching with parts of the body and the supposed four humors that had to be kept in balance in order to promote health. While he couldn't fully understand the mechanism without the other parts and their corresponding numbers, he knew enough to dial in what he wanted.

If only the mechanism had been complete.

"You've restored this like an expert," the thief said, his respect obvious in his voice. "It's almost as good as new. And the work you've done on these gears will make it run smoothly once I find the last piece."

Yes, he had spent many long hours painstakingly cleaning away the corrosion that had affected the piece after its long years in the ground. Sergio was proud of what he had done, proud of the research he had conducted even while slowly dying.

This was his mechanism, and this crude American with his swagger and his hammer had no right to take it.

With the strength of desperation, Sergio hauled himself to his feet, grabbed the hammer, and swung. The man had just enough time to turn in surprise.

But Sergio had used the last of his strength just in getting up. The hammer bounced lightly off the man's forehead, forcing a cry from him. He stumbled back as Sergio lost his balance and had to steady himself on the desk.

With a growl, the American set down the device, giving Sergio enough time to raise his arm for another swing.

He never got to make it. A strong hand grasped his wrist, twisted, and the hammer fell with a thud to the floor.

The American pushed him hard, and Sergio fell. For a moment he was disoriented, his lungs burned with the threat of another coughing fit, but then a sudden sharp awareness banished all thought of that.

The American stood over him, hammer in hand.

The hammer came down, and Sergio's vision burst into a brilliant light.

Pain. Disorientation. A last longing look at the edge of the device sticking out just within view over the side of the desk, and then the hammer came down again.

Sergio Ramon-Diaz's skull cracked, and his long suffering, and his long quest, both ended.

CHAPTER FOURTEEN

On the Mediterranean coast twenty kilometers east of Málaga, Spain

The next afternoon

Remi rubbed gritty eyes as she and Daniel sat in the back of a Spanish police car. Just a few hours before, Detective Chief Inspector Gupta had tracked down Sergio Ramon-Diaz via the Spanish antiquities office, where citizens had to get permits to import ancient artifacts. The office had given him Sergio's address, which they forwarded to the local police.

An hour later, they received the news that he had been found murdered.

Brian Edge wasn't the killer. Gupta found no record of his ever having been to Spain. The actual killer remained a step ahead of them, leaving a trail of bodies for them to follow.

She and Daniel took a middle-of the-night flight down here. It was the first plane they could catch, but even that was far too late to save Sergio Ramon-Diaz.

Three dead collectors. A search of Ramon-Diaz's home would almost certainly reveal his piece had been stolen. So three stolen pieces out of four. If the killer had the fourth piece, the trail would go cold. If someone else had it, there would be another murder.

They arrived in front of a large villa with stone walls and a sloping roof of red tiles. It stood at the end of a dirt road on a bluff overlooking the sea. Remi gazed out at the beautiful blue water under a matching sky puffed with the occasional cloud of bright white.

This was the kind of house that sold for millions, the patrolman who drove them here told her in passable French. But the man who had lived here had been too sick to enjoy it.

Sergio Ramon-Diaz had been a recluse and a collector, famous in Málaga's and Barcelona's collector circuit. The few who knew him said he was personable, but always reserved even before the illness stole his spirit and made him disappear from the openings and auctions that he used to never miss. The few parties he held were famous for their excellent catering, peerless guest list, and scintillating conversation. Everyone bemoaned the fact that there weren't more such parties, but the collector always seemed strained by the effort of such gatherings.

Others only saw Sergio from a distance, because he was a fixture at all such events, always immaculately dressed, always restrained in behavior, and always alone. He did not buy often, but when he did he always bought the most historically significant pieces, whether they were the most beautiful or best preserved or not, and he always managed to drive a hard bargain.

"I know this because my niece studied art restoration in the university," the patrolman said. "She worked for a year at the municipal museum, and now works at a gallery. She saw him at many functions."

That was all the patrolman knew, but Remi filed it away. Any extra information could be significant. As the patrol car came to a stop and Remi and her partner got out, she saw approaching a man who she hoped would have a lot more answers for her—the local inspector.

Inspector Juan de Fuca was, unlike most of his American counterparts, an immaculate dresser. A slim man in his fifties with slicked back salt and pepper hair, he wore a fine black wool overcoat over matching slacks and a dress shirt. His sharp eyes took in the two FBI agents as he strolled over and extended a hand to Daniel.

"Pleased to have you on board," he said in English with the barest trace of an accent. Then he turned to Remi and switched to equally good French. "I wasn't aware that the FBI was hiring non-Americans these days."

De Fuca gave her a kiss on each cheek in the Continental style. While second nature to Remi, she had grown unused to the gesture in her time in the United States, where people seemed to live inside an invisible bubble of personal space.

"What have you discovered so far?" Remi asked, switching back to English for Daniel's benefit.

"The coroner has come and gone. The victim was killed in the small hours of the morning. Blunt trauma to the head, probably from a hammer. We've swept the house for prints and hair samples. We are already in touch with Detective Chief Inspector Gupta in London and Detective Foster in Maryland. We'll see if we get any matches. Come."

The inspector led them into the house and through a tiled entryway and living room decorated with a few choice items of archaeological interest. Remi could see immediately that what the police officer had said on the way over had been correct. Sergio Ramon-Diaz had chosen artifacts based on historical importance rather than condition.

That statue by the doorway between the entry hall and the living room, for example, was a very early example of a Greek *kouros*, an athletic youth sculpted in marble around 600 B.C. It was battered, with half the face gone, but the general treatment remained visible enough to show that this was one of the first examples of that style of art in existence. Remi couldn't recall ever seeing one in such a developmental state.

Such an important piece really belonged in a museum. Despite her close ties to the world of collectors, it had always bothered her how the rich squirreled away rare artifacts of history for their own enjoyment. A piece of world heritage wasn't the same thing as a Rolex. That statue was everyone's property.

They passed through the living room, De Fuca gesturing at the sliding glass door leading to a patio overlooking the sea.

"There was no sign of forced entry, but that was unlocked. Your reports mention there was no forced entry in the other two murders?"

"That's correct," Daniel said. "The victims either invited them in or the killer was able to break in without leaving a trace."

"It is a simple matter to climb onto that balcony from the surrounding slope," the Spanish inspector said. "So if Señor Ramon-Diaz forgot to lock the back door, or was out getting some air, that would have been an easy entry point. And the victim would not have been able to resist. I spoke with the hospital. He had terminal cancer. His doctor begged him to enter a hospice, or at least to stop traveling, but he refused."

"He was still hunting for the device," Remi murmured.

"Yes, you mentioned this in your report," De Fuca said. "It would seem that the murderer got what he wanted."

They entered a study much like that of any academic, with extensive bookshelves and no other furnishings other than a chair, desk, and computer. Remi saw one difference, however. Most of the shelves didn't hold books, but chemically neutral conservation boxes, no doubt containing the victim's collection.

Two differences, Remi reminded herself. There was the chalk outline of a body on the floor, and a giant bloodstain on the tile.

Remi shuddered. Was she already getting so accustomed to this that her eye passed over such grisly details in favor of searching for clues?

Remi stepped over to an open box on the desk and found the padded interior empty.

He has at least three of the four pieces now. He might even have them all.

If he does, he'll stop killing. He'll simply disappear and we might never catch him.

Daniel came and stood next to her, looking down on the empty box. From the look on his face, she could tell he shared her concerns.

"Brian mentioned that Sergio thought this device would help him somehow," Daniel said. "The English collector seemed to agree. Any idea what they were talking about?"

"No. The only photos I've seen were from the Greek excavation from several years ago. The artifacts were fresh out of the ground. It was impossible to see if there was any writing that would give us a clue as to its purpose, and I haven't heard of any ancient Greek device that supposedly had healing properties. The Greeks used herbal medicine and diet to cure people, not clockwork mechanisms."

"Maybe this is something the historians don't know about. Some sort of magical device. The Church didn't preserve a lot of the old Greek magical texts because they were pagan."

Remi nodded. Despite their being a wealth of textual and archaeological evidence about the Classical world, there was still so much they did not know.

But Sergio Ramon-Diaz would have known. Judging from his collection, he was an expert, and she saw a set of restoration tools on one shelf. The killer's latest victim had probably known everything there was to know about the device.

So where did he keep that information?

Remi took a slow turn about the room, keeping clear of the body outline on the floor and studying each shelf. She saw no notebooks. The computer no doubt held files on his collection, and those would have to be searched, but she suspected that Sergio would have kept any information on the device in a more secure place. He had been old enough to not fully trust or feel comfortable with computers. All the older academics she knew still preferred keeping things on paper.

If I wanted to hide the information that might save my life, where would I put it?

Remi stopped and stared at the shelves again. The longer one, running the length of the longer wall in this rectangular room, was mostly taken up by conservation boxes, including the one that had been taken out of its spot and placed on the desk. A few books sat there as well. Using her Italian to puzzle out the Spanish titles, the two languages being closely related, she saw they were mostly on the restoration and care of ancient artifacts.

She moved to the shorter shelf on the far end of the study, filled with books in Spanish, Latin, and ancient Greek. A large, leather-bound volume of the *Corpus Hippocraticum* caught her eye. This was a collection of some sixty early medical texts attributed to Hippocrates, possibly first assembled by researchers in the Library of Alexandria.

Remi pulled it off the shelf. Sergio might have marked parts of the text, or put notes in the margins that could give her a clue as to the device's intended function.

She opened the book, and her jaw dropped.

The leather cover, looking so professionally printed, was a ruse. There wasn't a book inside.

There was a notebook.

Pages upon pages of neat handwriting, diagrams, and charts. Pasted to one page were the photographs of the device from the original excavation, and after these were pasted the pages from the field report describing the context of the find. Other pages had long quotes from ancient Greek medical texts.

She flipped forward, and found a close-up photograph of one of the pieces, a circular plate with a couple of corroded gears fixed to the front. Beyond this came another photograph of the same piece after restoration. Remi could clearly see the numbers on the gears, and the Greek text along the edge of the plate. But she didn't have to squint to read these, because the next page contained an expertly done sketch of the plate clearer than any photograph.

She turned to the next page, and there she found taped to the paper a business card.

“Jan Horvat, rare antiquities”

Below that was an address in Ljubljana, the capital of Slovenia in Eastern Europe, and an email address and phone number.

“What have you found?” Daniel asked, coming up next to her.

“Everything,” Remi whispered. “I think I’ve found everything.”

CHAPTER FIFTEEN

Remi sat in the living room, poring over the notebook while Daniel looked up the antiquities dealer named in the business card. He had brought along his laptop and was using the dead man's WIFI. Perhaps this lead might give him justice.

And the notebook would give her insight into why he was killed.

It was fascinating and bizarre reading, part historical detective work, part masterpiece of research and reconstruction, spiced with a dash of sheer madness. It took her down strange avenues of Greek medicine and magic, and an esoteric tradition she had never heard of before.

She was so focused on her reading that she didn't notice Daniel standing by her until he tapped her on the shoulder.

"We're going to Ljubljana," he said. "Turns out Jan Horvat is quite the international superstar."

"How so?"

Daniel held up his laptop so she could see a file photo of a middle-aged Slavic man with a shaved head and arrogant blue eyes.

"Before Slovenia broke away from the old Yugoslavia in 1991, and the rest of the country disintegrated into civil war the next year, Horvat was a young secret service officer. Slovenian by birth but loyal to the old regime, probably because that was the best way to climb the ladder. When all that went away, he took advantage of the chaos of the civil war to run guns into the conflict zone and refugees out of it. For a charge, of course. The antiquities dealing seems to be a new thing, a legal company to launder money and give him a respectable façade."

"But he's selling stolen antiquities too."

"Probably. He hasn't been investigated for that because there's more important things to watch him for."

"Drugs?"

"No, still the guns. While the civil war is over, Balkan mafias have spread all across Europe. Our friend De Fuca could tell us how the drug imports into Madrid are handled by the Moroccans and the Albanians.

In other Spanish cities it's the Russians or Romanians. This is the same in a dozen countries. They have a foothold everywhere, and in some places they dominate. Much of the gun violence in Europe is actually the fault of these gangs."

Remi nodded. When she was a child, her policeman father hardly ever had to deal with a shooting. Now shootings were fairly common. Not nearly as bad as in the United States, but still shocking to European sensibilities.

"How did you find this out?" Remi asked.

"A bit of interagency liaising. An old college buddy of mine joined the CIA. He got me the information."

"The CIA is investigating Horvat?"

"The CIA keeps tabs on all international gun running. These Eastern European gangs are a pretty big threat to overseas interests, plus they're worried he might sell guns to terrorists."

"Why haven't they arrested him?"

"No evidence. He's smart. Slovenia is the most stable of all the former Yugoslav states. It avoided the worst of the civil war and developed a proper democracy without any of the nasty nationalism you see in some of the other nations. He uses that as a shelter, plus he's very good at covering his tracks. But now," Daniel gestured at the notebook, "we have sufficient cause to get the local police to bust in and search his warehouse. What have you discovered?"

"So much!" Remi enthused. She had been bursting to share what she had discovered. "This device was simpler than the Antikythera mechanism, but highly specialized in a different way. As I suspected, not all of the mechanism has survived, although the main parts have. Sergio Ramon-Diaz did some masterful reconstruction work, and while some of it is hypothetical, I think he was one hundred percent correct."

"Correct about what?" Daniel said with a note of impatience. He always got a bit fussy if she didn't get to the point right away, but she wanted to communicate to him just how important this find, and its reconstruction, could be.

"The plate that was stolen was the base, and the main dial. Various other gears finetuned the mechanism and put varying pressure on a spring that, when released, would strike a thin metal tube, probably of gold, that would then resonate at a particular frequency depending on the tension in the various gears. It's not just a complex set of gearworks, but also a finely turned musical instrument."

"A musical instrument?"

"One ancient Greek mystical tradition held that sound could affect health. The right sounds could restore the balance of the four humors that made up the body. Imbalances in these humors created all illness other than physical injury, and so Ramon-Diaz theorized that properly tuned and pointed at the affected area, this device could cure any disease."

"He thought he could cure his cancer by shooting certain notes at his body with an ancient mechanism?"

"Yes."

"That's stupid."

Remi paused. On the surface, it did sound stupid, but to a researcher steeped in ancient mysticism facing a painful death? It sounded more like the last hope.

"Stupid or not, it was Sergio Ramon-Diaz's motivation for buying on the illegal antiquities market. Grayson and Brentford were both getting on in years and probably had underlying health issues. That's why they tried to assemble the device too."

"And our killer is probably the same. But he's shown physical strength and prowess. This isn't some escapee from a hospice," Daniel said.

"Perhaps he has some manageable condition like AIDS, or a family member is sick."

"Maybe. The problem is, we still have no idea who this guy is."

"No," Remi said, snapping the notebook shut and standing, "and that's why we need to raid our good friend Jan Horvat in Slovenia."

* * *

It wasn't until that evening that they managed to get to Ljubljana, the capital of Slovenia. Remi had managed to sleep a bit on the plane but still felt groggy from the jetlag she had never had time to banish.

It didn't matter. She'd been to enough airports to steer through security and baggage pickup on automatic. What she didn't expect were the two young men waiting for them at the exit.

They were supposed to be met by a pair of local CIA operatives, but the men holding the sign saying "Daniel Walker" looked anything but.

Firstly, they didn't look a day over twenty-five. Both wore the loose but sturdy khaki pants and boots favored by hikers, and colorful wool tops imported from South America. Both had scraggly beards.

Remi let Daniel take the lead. He'd been the one liaising with the CIA.

He walked up to the two men. "I'm Daniel Walker."

"Good to meet you!" the one not carrying the sign gave him a fist bump. "Ready for some awesome hiking?"

"Sure am," Daniel said, not missing a beat. He gestured at his suit. "Don't worry, I have my hiking clothes in my bag. So does my wife."

Wife! Remi blushed. Well, they *were* undercover.

They departed the terminal to a waiting four-by-four that had sides spattered with dried mud. Once they got in, the operatives' tone changed immediately.

"We've put a tracker on Horvat's vehicle and it looks like he's heading to a warehouse he rented a few Klicks outside town. We need to rendezvous with someone before we go."

Remi wondered what he meant by "clicks" but felt too embarrassed to ask. Did they have some special odometer that clicked with each kilometer?

The car took them through winding, well-lit streets lined with nineteenth-century stone buildings. A church spire rose to one side. Beyond, atop a hug outcropping of rock, floodlights lit up a castle.

"So tell us the situation," Remi said.

"We've been monitoring Horvat for a couple of years. The antiquities thing is pretty new, and to be honest we never thought that would give us a reason to bust him, so thanks for the help. We've got indications that he's running guns and ammo, but it's all just hearsay and rumor. Nothing solid to get the green light from the Slovenian authorities."

"So the local P.D. is on board with this?" Daniel asked.

"Now they are. They needed probable cause. Slovenia is one of the few countries in this area to emerge from the Cold War without much crime and gangsterism."

Remi suppressed a smile. The Cold War ended before these two young men were even born.

"How long have you been assigned to Slovenia?" Remi asked.

"Three years," the driver replied, making Remi wonder if she had underestimated their age. "The cover is that we're two expats supporting ourselves by teaching English and running hiking and skiing tours. When this is all over, we'd love to take you on a hike in the Slovenian Alps. Just as beautiful as the Bavarian Alps but a hell of a lot cheaper."

Daniel laughed. "Can it compete with Switzerland or the Dolomites?"

"Nope," the driver said, giving him a youthful grin through the rearview mirror. "We don't mention that on the website."

Remi glanced at her partner. Had he been to those places? He seemed to have traveled quite a lot—he certainly had some nuggets of knowledge born of travel—and yet never mentioned it. The truth just slipped out sometimes.

The CIA agent in the passenger seat looked over his shoulder at them.

"The man we're going to meet can provide you with a firearm each. What do you folks use over there at the FBI? Glocks?"

"We have ours," Daniel said.

The man's eyebrows shot up. "The Antiquities Division gets to take their firearms overseas? You got some high connections in D.C."

Daniel and Remi only nodded. It was strange how well-connected such a new and underfunding department had turned out to be. While Remi was no expert in American politics, it was obvious someone was pulling strings for them. Their last case had even sent them into a warzone.

But why?

Remi suppressed a shudder as she remembered a harrowing incident on the highway to Axum when they got caught near the front line of a battle in that country's civil war.

And now she was going to face gunplay again.

Remi turned to look out the window, her eyes barely registering the small cobblestone squares and orderly houses, or the trees in the hills behind looking yellow in the harsh streetlights. They were already at the outskirts of the capital, and Remi could felt herself tensing up.

It hadn't been so bad going to intercept the groundskeeper making his deal, because she couldn't be sure someone would pull a gun. Now she was sure. Two CIA agents calling for backup and handing out guns was a very bad sign.

And suddenly, for the first time in many years, Remi Laurent doubted her ability to do the job. She had been in a couple of gunfights already and hadn't performed as well as she had hoped. She found them confusing, noise everywhere, people moving so quickly, and you never knew just when was the right time to shoot, or even if you should shoot.

And now she had to do this with Eastern European gunrunners? They were probably all veterans of the various wars in the Balkans. Even Daniel would be out of his depth.

And herself? Pure madness to go along with this. She wasn't qualified. She wasn't trained. What was she doing here?

"You OK?" Daniel asked in a soft voice.

She shook off her thoughts and turned to her partner. He looked back at her, the streetlights illuminating his open expression of concern.

Remi simply nodded, not trusting herself to speak. She didn't want the casual-but-no-doubt-capable CIA operatives in the front seat to judge her.

"We'll stick together and let the heavies do the main fighting," Daniel told her.

Daniel's hand slid across the back seat. Remi took it gratefully, their fingers intertwining. They had gotten out of the city now and it was dark in the car. The CIA agents wouldn't see. She didn't want them judging her for this either.

Judging for what, exactly?

Nothing. He's getting back with his wife. This is just him reassuring me. Nothing more.

Men reassure women with words, not by holding hands.

Unless they ...

Stop it. You have a fight to deal with.

A few kilometers from the edge of town, down a secondary two-lane road, the CIA men pulled off onto a small lot in front of a garage. One of the doors was up to show a tow truck parked inside, a logo painted on the side. A burly man in coveralls came out. He looked about thirty, with a thick black beard trimmed short, and a solid frame that nevertheless moved with an easy grace.

"Here's our contact," the driver said.

Remi nodded at the sense of it. A tow truck wouldn't excite curiosity anywhere, and in the country, neither would a pair of clueless-looking American hikers.

The operative on the passenger side rolled down his window as the bigger man sauntered up and leaned his forearm against the door. He barely glanced at the two FBI agents in the back.

"They're armed," the driver told the two truck operator, "and we brought our pieces."

The man gave a curt nod. "I'll go in front. You follow about a hundred yards behind. When we get to the village, we'll park in front of the bar and walk the rest of the way. The local team is waiting for us at the rendezvous."

"All right."

The tow truck man looked right at Remi, as if appraising her and not liking what he saw.

Not sure of the one woman in the group? Go to hell.

Although I do *feel unsure of myself. And I'm* not *qualified for this job, damn it!*

Without a word, the man pushed off from the car and sauntered back to his tow truck.

"We'll be there in fifteen minutes," the driver said, looking at them in the rearview mirror. "It's a small town, just a few shops by the side of the road and some houses behind. There's a bar there we can park at and the warehouse is less than a kilometer up the road. We'll walk. Gus has some heavy weapons. We'll be all right just with side arms."

The two truck pulled away and the driver got back on to the road, keeping well behind.

Fifteen minutes, Remi thought. Fifteen minutes and I'll be under fire again.

CHAPTER SIXTEEN

They walked in silence, the mechanic taking point with an assault rifle wrapped in a blanket tucked under his arm. The other CIA agents had UZIs hidden under their windbreakers. Remi, walking a little behind with Daniel, kept touching the butt of her pistol, hiding under a thin sweater, for reassurance.

The driver had called it a town, but it barely qualified as a hamlet. Remi tried to control her breathing as they walked up the darkened country road, leaving the few lights of the bar, convenience store, and about ten houses behind them. The air felt sharp, clean, and cool. Slovenia was a mountainous country and Remi guessed they were at a fairly high altitude. The road curved and rose, and soon the last of the lights disappeared behind them. Now they walked in darkness under an overcast sky. No cars passed on the two-lane road. Just as well since there wasn't a shoulder. Trees and underbrush grew close to the pavement, forcing them to keep to the edge.

At a point on the road that looked like any other, the lead man cut off into the woods. The others followed.

They slipped through the trees, the CIA men making no noise at all, the two FBI agents trying and failing to keep quiet. It was hard enough to sneak through the woods in the daytime, and here it was almost pitch dark. Remi and Daniel kept making the underbrush swish against their legs, and crunched leaves underfoot with almost every step. The lead man turned back to look at them a couple of times, and even though Remi couldn't see his face, she could sense his annoyance.

She peered through the trees, the feeble light of a waning crescent moon the only illumination. As they came to a clearing, Remi's heart clenched as she saw half a dozen dark figures standing there.

Her hand went to her gun, then froze as the lead CIA man raised a hand and said something in Slovenian. One of the figures, she couldn't tell who, replied, and the men fell in with their group.

This must be the local police, she thought. Remi could just make out the guns and uniforms. She wondered what the operative had told them. Had he revealed his work with the CIA, or presented some fake documents saying he worked with some other branch of government. He could have even claimed to be FBI.

Remi didn't know. None of the CIA people had bothered to fill them in.

They moved on, the sweat that had poured from her a moment before chilling her skin in the crisp mountain air.

Within a minute they saw lights ahead. One of the policemen made a gesture and three of the officers moved off to the left, while two more moved to the right. The darkness swallowed them within moments.

The rest of the group moved forward. At her side, Daniel pulled his gun. Licking her dry lips and trying to keep her hands from shaking, Remi did the same.

The trees thinned out, and before them loomed the blank side of a warehouse. Lights shone at the front of the building to their left, and a small light, perhaps for a back door, also shone around the corner to their right. No one was in sight and the wall facing them had no windows.

She scanned for security cameras and saw none, although she couldn't be sure in the poor light.

The CIA men and the lone Slovenian police officer, who Remi could now see had gold shoulder braids that probably denoted he was of higher rank, jogged over to the wall and pressed themselves against it. Remi and Daniel followed. She felt lke she was playing pretend soldier, with an emphasis on the "pretend."

With slow and deliberate steps, they moved toward the front of the warehouse. As they got to the corner, they could see a gravel lot in front with several parked cars, four-by-fours, and a van with no back windows. In the darkened tree line, they could just make out the three officers that had gone ahead, one busy handcuffing a burly man.

"He must have been standing guard," Daniel whispered. "These guys must be good at sneaking around if they got the jump on him."

And I'm not. I don't belong here.

The lead CIA operative, assault rifle in hand, quickly moved to a door standing next to the large garage door. Both were closed.

He got on one side of the door, while one of the younger operatives got on the other, looking somewhat ridiculous clutching a 9mm automatic while dressed like a hippie. Everyone arranged themselves to one side of the door, out of the direct line of fire and guns leveled. The lead man nodded, and the hiker tried the doorknob, nodded back, and then flung the door open.

Before Remi was ready, the battle was on. The two CIA agents rushed in, followed by a swarm of other men. Remi hesitated for half a second and found herself in the back of the line, with the second young CIA agent between her and Daniel.

By the time she made it through the door, the firing had already started.

And, as with every other gunfight she'd been in, confusion reigned.

The men had spread out, some moving forward and firing beside a parked truck while others ducked to the left to go around it. A quick glance showed a well-lit interior with a pair of trucks parked side by side. Behind the trucks stood stacks of wooden crates. That's all she got to register before a bullet hummed by her ear, making her duck.

She crouched beside the front tire of the truck, looking around, but could see none of the criminals. Her own people blocked the view.

A bullet crashed into the sideview mirror above her head, making her fall prone as she got showered with glass.

As she hugged the concrete floor, she looked left, under the truck, and straight into the wide-eyed face of an older Slavic man in a tracksuit.

Their eyes locked. For a moment, nothing, then both moved at once.

The older man leveled a revolver at her. Remi sprang up and back to get the heavy tire between her and the gunrunner, firing off an unaimed shot beneath the truck as she did so.

An instant later, the criminal fired back, his shot ringing out as it hit the inside hub of the tire.

Remi kept moving, bending low and reaching around the front end of the tire to fire again. Another blind shot, but being so close she didn't dare expose herself.

No return shot came. Remi summoned her courage and, as the shots from the surrounding gunfight reverberated off the corrugated steel roof and concrete walls to savage her eardrums, she peeked around the tire.

The gunrunner had disappeared, leaving only a trail of blood behind him.

I hit him.

Remi felt a cold flush of … something. Nausea? Fear? Disgust? Satisfaction?

Maybe all these things. But she didn't have time to sort out her emotions. As if on automatic, she ran around the truck and saw the trail of blood pass across the two meters of concrete floor between the trucks before disappearing under the second vehicle.

She darted across the open space between the trucks, expecting to have her legs shot out from under her, and once again got behind meager cover of the front tire.

Remi darted a glance around the tire, leading with her gun, and saw the blood trail move under the truck and out of sight on the other side.

A rattle of gunfire to her right made her look. A man in dirty jeans and a pullover ran past the far end of the two trucks, firing behind him as he went. Remi raised her gun but before she could fire her pirouetted, blood spurting from his shoulder, and staggered out of sight.

Beyond that, she could see stacks of crates arranged in rows. Flashes from gunshots behind them told her part of the battle had moved in there.

She looked around again, and for the moment saw she was alone.

That terrified her more than facing an enemy. Remi rounded the front of the truck and stopped short. Sitting with his back to the wall, clutching his bloody side with drenched hands, was one of the younger CIA agents. A man she didn't recognize lay dead nearby, a gun still in his hand.

Ahead she saw a half open door to an office. The blood trail from the man she had shot passed this and disappeared into the maze of crates at the back of the warehouse.

A man dashed between two stacks of crates. By the time she registered it was a stranger and had raised her gun, he had disappeared.

She glanced back at the wounded CIA man, who weakly gestured for her to move on, then clutched his wound again.

There was nothing she could do for him. She hadn't yet had her first aid training, and she didn't have any bandages. Remi faced forward, gun leveled, and squared her shoulders. Slowly she advanced on the stacks of crates, gunfire still raging from that hidden side of the warehouse.

Another man in a tracksuit appeared in the gap between the crates. He fired at something unseen. Remi aimed, and just as he turned to face her, eyes widening with surprise, she squeezed the trigger.

The bullet cracked off the crate nearest him, spraying him with splinters. His hand went up to his eye, and before Remi could fire again he jumped out of sight.

Remi paced forward again. A strange calm had settled on her. She had wounded two of the Slavic mafia and hadn't been hurt herself. She was all right. She could do this.

She got to where the door to her left stood half open. While the main fight lay ahead, she had learned enough from her accelerated FBI training not to leave an uncleared room behind her.

Edging to the wall while trying to keep an eye on both the crates and the doorway, she moved closer to the opening. The rattle of gunfire had died down a bit, but her ears still rang and she couldn't hear anything beyond that door.

Nothing to do but burst in and check.

Taking a deep breath, she rushed into the room while shouting, "FBI! Hands up!"

She kicked the door wide and swiveled to the right. Nothing. She shifted to look left …

… and stopped as she felt the cold muzzle of a gun pressed against her temple.

CHAPTER SEVENTEEN

"Don't make a move," a voice said in English with a thick Slavic accent. "Drop the gun."

Remi let go of the gun and it fell to the carpeted floor with a thump.

She stood in an office. A filing cabinet to her right. Opposite her, a desk and an older desktop PC. To her left … she didn't dare turn that direction.

"Step forward," the voice ordered.

She took a couple of steps forward, getting out of sight of the doorway and any possible help. Gunfire continued in the warehouse. She had no idea who was winning or losing. Did it even matter now, at least as far as she was concerned?

"I … I am an officer of the American FBI. If you kill me they will execute you."

She didn't think that was true, but maybe it might help save her life.

"I knew you were coming sooner or later. Turn around."

Remi turned, and found herself facing Jan Horvat. She recognized him from his file photo. He wore a conservative business suit that would have made him look like an attorney or financial advisor except for the .357 Magnum he gripped in his hand.

"You are here because of the murders. Because of Grayson and Ramon-Diaz. I always keep an eye out for news about my customers. They have both been murdered for the Greek pieces."

"Why are you telling me this?" Remi asked.

There was a pause. Remi realized she didn't hear any more firing. A shout in Slovenian was answered with a reply in the same language. From the look on Horvat's face, his side had not won.

I hope Daniel is all right.

"I am telling you for insurance. Because I did not kill them. I think I know who did."

"Who?"

"Another man who was interested in the device. He said he had a piece he wanted to sell. I do not know if he had it or simply knew where to get it. I will tell you who this man is, and you will let me walk away."

Remi paused. She needed to get that information, but she knew she couldn't make such a promise.

Horvat glared at her. "Make this deal or I walk away with you as hostage."

Remi opened her mouth to speak.

Just then, Daniel burst in. Horvat turned, too late. Daniel's gun barked, and Horvat flew back, blood spurting from his chest, to bang against the desk, his back slamming into the computer screen and cracking it.

Horvat stumbled, dropped his gun, and fell flat on his face.

* * *

An hour later at the hospital, the CIA agent posing as a tow truck operator, who nursed a bandage on his cheek from a grazing wound, told them Horvat was in critical condition and could not be questioned for some time.

Remi and Daniel sat on uncomfortable plastic chairs in the hallway, near a nervous woman who prayed softly to herself in Slovenian. Remi wondered what horrible news awaited her.

"Sorry you're not getting further in your case," the operative said. "But at least we busted him and his gang. We found twenty AK-47s in that warehouse along with a box of grenades. Horvat is going to wake up to a long prison sentence."

"How is your man?" Remi asked.

"Stabilized. He lost a lot of blood but he'll pull through. No hikes for him this month, though. At least he can drop that granola hippie act for a while."

One of the Slovenian police officers had also sustained a gunshot wound, but it had only been a graze to the hand.

"And the gang members?" Remi asked.

Two of the gang members had been killed and several more wounded.

The CIA operative shrugged. "The head surgeon says all of them will pull through. Too bad. A bigger body count would have sent a clearer message."

Remi's relief at the first half of his statement got replaced by stomach churning disgust at the second half.

The operative extended a hand. Remi and Daniel both shook it. Remi resisted the urge to wipe her hand on her slacks.

"Nice bit of interagency cooperation we had," he said with a smile. "Now if you'll excuse me I have to go. Gunfights always mean a mountain of paperwork."

He turned and walked away down the hall. Remi watched him go.

"What a terrible world that man lives in. Imagine actually *wanting* a higher body count."

Daniel clicked his tongue. "Don't shed a tear for those mafia types. They deal in death. Many of them traffic women too."

Remi grimaced. "They all deserve to go to jail for the rest of their lives. But killing them?"

Daniel looked her in the eye, and she saw that hardness she had glimpsed a few times before.

"They're evil, and sometimes to fight evil you have to kill evil. That's what you signed on for, Remi. That's why you're getting firearms training. This hasn't been your first gunfight and it won't be your last. You need to get used to that."

Remi shuddered and looked away.

Daniel rested a hand on hers and their fingers naturally interlaced. In a softer tone, he went on.

"I know it's an adjustment. A big one. You've had a pretty sheltered life. Maybe I'm wrong, but I'm thinking you've never had to face evil until now. Even so, you got something in you that's driving you to come over and see the darker side that people like us and that crazy guy who just left have to deal with. I don't know what made you switch careers, but this isn't just about puzzle solving and hunting down ancient artifacts."

"I know that," Remi replied, somewhat annoyed, both at Daniel and at herself. At Daniel for lecturing her on what she already knew, and at herself for her bad habit of forgetting those facts.

Her annoyance shifted to curiosity as she looked down at Daniel's fingers interlaced with her own. This was the third time he had done this, and she had allowed it as if it was natural and normal.

But this wasn't. He was a coworker, with an ex-wife he was trying to get back together with, so why was he doing this? It wasn't simple reassurance. He'd done that numerous times before without having to touch her, and he wasn't a very physical person with his friends or other coworkers. None of the slaps on the backs or man hugs some of the other agents engaged in. No, this was new.

Her going along with it was also new. As a woman in academia, she had fended off countless attempts at physical contact with her male colleagues. She wasn't as prickly as some of the female professors she knew in the United States—who would be enraged if a man tried to give them the traditional French kiss on both cheeks—but she had developed an enforced personal space as part of her career-long push for respect.

And here was this uncouth divorcee breaking it.

And at least at an unconscious level, he knew what he was doing. He only touched her when other people weren't looking. Like in the back of the dark car going to Horvat's warehouse. Or here in the hall, after the one person they knew had left.

Remi knew she should pull back her hand. Search in her pockets or check her phone or something else that would mask the movement as ordinary and unplanned, but she didn't.

Because she didn't want to.

Why didn't she want to?

Remi realized Daniel was talking.

" … and it's too bad we didn't get to question him. He really seemed to want to spill to you to get himself off the hook. I bet he thought murdering an American millionaire would get him more time than running guns. Or that giving you information would get him a deal. That's usually how those characters think. Always an angle with guys like that. I just wish I didn't have to shoot him."

Remi sighed. "Without him, I don't know how we're going to proceed with the investigation. He was our only lead. He couldn't have murdered the three victims, because one of the CIA men told me he's been in the country for the past several weeks."

"He could have hired a hitman," Daniel said.

"Then why admit that he knew two of the victims? You'd think he'd deny everything and hide behind an expensive lawyer. Strange that he didn't mention Brentford. Why not? Does that mean he only sold two of the pieces and Brentford got his from someone else? Damn it! How are we going to move forward now?"

Daniel gave her hand a squeeze. She looked up at him and their eyes met.

"I'm sorry I had to shoot him," Daniel said, his voice wavering. "It sets the investigation back, I know. It's just that when I came into that office and saw him holding a gun to your head, I … I just couldn't let him hurt you."

"You did what you had to do," she said softly. "I don't blame you."

Remi found she herself squeezing Daniel's hand. Suddenly embarrassed, she pulled away …

… and then leaned forward.

Without plan, without thought, she drew closer to Daniel, eyes hooded, chin upraised, lips pushing ever so slightly outward.

Daniel's phone buzzed, snapping her out of her near-hypnotic trance.

Daniel didn't move. His face remained only centimeters from hers. She could feel his warm breath.

His phone buzzed again.

With exaggerated haste, he pulled it out of his pocket, turning slightly away as he checked it. Remi pulled back …

… but not before seeing who had texted him.

Veronica. His ex-wife.

Guilt washed over her, made worse by how much Daniel was blushing and avoiding her gaze.

"I need to get this," he mumbled.

"Right."

Remi sprang up and walked down the hall.

CHAPTER EIGHTEEN

Daniel opened his messages. Veronica had sent two.

"How is Spain? I hope you're getting some sun and sangria along with the murder investigation!"

An oddly chipper remark from his ex, and one that made him somewhat annoyed. Actually her messaging him at this particular moment made him super annoyed.

Because Remi had been about to …

You're married, nitwit.

No, you're not. Veronica dumped you. You're as free as you want to be.

Come on, she's trying to make amends. She never made light of your cases before. She's trying to accept your career for once.

The message also reminded him that he hadn't told her he had switched countries. It gave truth to her old complaint, "I never know where you are, and I never know when you're coming back!"

With that gunfight, I almost didn't come back. Neither did Remi.

God, when I saw that creep pointing a gun at her head ...

With a conscious effort, he pushed the thought of his partner out of his mind and read Veronica's second message.

"When you pass through duty free, get a nice bottle of Spanish red. We can have it over dinner when you come back. ☺"

Daniel took in a sharp breath. So far, their meetings had suffered from a weird kind of formality. They'd meet in a café or some other crowded place, insurance against either of them losing their cool, and would talk about general things like work and the news. It was almost like going out for coffee with a coworker you didn't know very well and weren't sure you liked.

Now she was talking about a date. More than a date, an old tradition.

Both of them had busy professional lives, and so during their marriage they would sometimes schedule a "date", a night when they would order a delivery from one of the nicer restaurants in town, splurge on a good bottle of wine, and eat at home. These dates usually ended in a long session of lovemaking.

Those dates were some of Daniel's fondest memories of his marriage, made more precious by their rarity. Veronica's job as a senior manager at a large corporation often meant she had to stay late to handle one crisis or another, and Daniel's cases pulled him along like a marionette on a string. So Daniel could probably count their dates on two hands.

Dinner ... fine wine ... what comes after ... She's really trying to get me back.

So why does that scare the crap out of me? This is what I want, after all.

Right?

Daniel had never wanted to get divorced. It had all been her idea. Veronica said he was too obsessed with his work. Fair point, but when lives were on the line, how couldn't he be obsessed? If she screwed up, the quarterly report would contain errors or the company would miss out on some contract. If he screwed up, an innocent person would die a horrible death at the hands of some psycho.

And then there was the issue of children. He couldn't have them. Low sperm count. Why? The doctors didn't know. Veronica, after hitting a glass ceiling at work, had shifted her life a bit away from her career and now wanted to have kids. Daniel wanted to adopt. She didn't. An insolvable problem they never really discussed.

So how would this date fix anything?

Still, it was an olive branch. He should take it.

Veronica wanted to get back with him. That's what he had wanted all along.

So why did he keep thinking about Remi?

Get your head straight, Daniel. Flirting with your partner is totally unprofessional. You got a killer to hunt down.

Lost in his thoughts, it took him a full minute before he noticed an earlier message on his phone, one he hadn't heard because it had come while they had been approaching Horvat's warehouse and he had put his phone on silent.

This came from Assistant Director Ochiai.

"I need a status update. Your travel funds have risen quite high and the Resource Allocation people are complaining. There have been cuts to the agency travel budget. Have you made progress in Slovenia?"

Daniel groaned. Tonight he had planned to type up a report on the fight in the warehouse. Two CIA agents injured, their covers probably blown, and while they had nabbed a bunch of gunrunners, they had done nothing to get closer to the case, thanks to his being trigger happy.

Like he had any choice! Remi had gotten herself into trouble again. While she was the most knowledgeable and useful trainee he had ever seen, she had a talent for impulsively getting herself into situations that required him to save her.

Daniel texted back, "We arrested Horvat in a combined operation with the local police and the CIA operatives I mentioned in my last message. Horvat was seriously injured and in no condition to be questioned. Full report coming tonight."

He sent it and winced. That wouldn't go over well. Ochiai wanted results. The bean counters at Resource Allocation wanted results. And he wasn't delivering results.

This reminded him just how perilous his position was at the FBI. He had been demoted to this new unit, and the higher-ups had probably been waiting for him to fail so they could stick him in some desk job. Despite this, he and Remi had solved four cases in rapid succession. Was that enough to please them? Hell, no! Now they were complaining about a few hotels and plane tickets.

Daniel got to work on the report, trying to figure out how to make a dead-end in the case not look like … well … a dead end.

Otherwise, his career would be at a dead end.

* * *

Flustered and sitting in her hotel room, Remi struggled to concentrate. Their investigation had reached an impasse, Daniel said the assistant director was clamoring for results, and they had no idea where to turn to next.

For all they knew, the killer might have all four pieces by now. He or she may never kill again, and the faint trail they had been following would soon grow cold.

So she went back to what she was accustomed to—examining historical texts.

In this case, the notebook she had found in the house of the Spanish victim. He seemed to have done the most research on the device, or at least had done her the courtesy of writing it all down.

The problem was, being a personal notebook, it proved difficult to figure out. Like her own notes, they were written for herself and not for the outside reader, and so contained many references she didn't understand. Also, many of the quotes from ancient sources weren't cited, an amateurish omission you wouldn't get from a real scholar.

It also didn't help that it was mostly written in Spanish. She was fluent in French and Italian, both languages being close, so that helped, but it still made for slow going.

She had been at it for hours, and hadn't found out anything new except the depth of Sergio Ramon-Diaz's research.

Fascinating reading, but it didn't bring her any closer to getting him any justice.

Remi rubbed her eyes and adjusted her position as she sat on the bed, two pillows propping up her back. This was exhausting. How long had it been since she had gotten a full night of sleep? She certainly hadn't caught up with her jetlag.

You haven't caught up with the murderer either.

She kept reading. Still she didn't find anything that would help her.

Frustrated, she turned back to the first page. Maybe she had missed something at the start, a synthesis or a reference to source material.

On the flyleaf, Remi noticed something strange amid all the scribbled notes—a line that wasn't in Ramon-Diaz's handwriting. It was also in blue ink instead of the predominant black.

"Buena suerte, tak for mad!

"V.C."

Remi stared at the line. *Buena suerte* meant "good luck" in Spanish, but what about the rest of the sentence? That didn't look like Spanish.

She got onto Google, typed in "take for mad", and learned that it was a common expression in Danish, used to thank someone for buying them a meal.

Why would someone write a sentence half in Spanish and half in Danish in Ramon-Diaz's journal? And what about "V.C."? Was that the person's initials?

It seemed that this was someone familiar with the victim, someone friendly and trusted enough to be allowed to write in the journal, play with two languages, and sign only with his or her initials.

Remi thought back to Ramon-Diaz's study and library, trying to remember if she had seen any Danish-language books there. She didn't think so, but then again she hadn't made an exhaustive search.

Remi recalled seeing a few other notes in blue ink. She started flipping through pages, and found here and there amid Ramon-Diaz's research check marks in blue ink, and a couple of spots where the other person had corrected Ramon-Diaz's rendering of Ancient Greek. While it was difficult to tell with such a different alphabet, the Greek writing appeared to be by the same hand as the note in Spanish and Danish.

She checked the corrections, and found they had been done by someone with a deep knowledge of the language. While Ramon-Diaz's knowledge was the best she'd ever seen in a layman, the corrections were on another level entirely.

Remi put the journal on her lap and stared at the blank wall of her hotel room. Someone with the initials V.C. who knew Spanish, Danish, and Ancient Greek. There couldn't be that many of those in the world.

But how to find them?

The answer hit her like a thunderbolt. She knew who it might be!

Viggo Christensen was a professor of Classical Archaeology at the University of Copenhagen. A renowned expert on Ancient Greek, he was also known for his writings on the Antikythera mechanism and other early Greek mechanical devices.

Did he speak Spanish too? Remi wasn't sure. At conferences he had spoken to her in good French, used fluent English in his talks, and as a Classicist he surely spoke Italian. Remi had noted that the less useful a scholar's native language was, the more languages they tended to speak. Scandinavian scholars were especially known for this. Viggo Christensen spoke English better than most Americans.

But was this really the right person?

She fired off an email to Inspector Juan De Fuca, asking him to check airline records to see if Christensen had visited Spain, or if Ramon-Diaz had flown to Denmark.

As she waited for a response, she checked an online database of Classical historians, archaeologists, and professors of ancient languages. She could find no one with the initials V.C. except for a professor of Sanskrit named Vikram Chakrabarty. He didn't strike her as a likely suspect.

The search took her fifteen minutes. A shower and getting ready for bed took another twenty. By the time she checked her phone, De Fuca had answered. He had already pulled Ramon-Diaz's travel records earlier that day.

The Spanish collector had flown to Copenhagen for a five-day visit several months ago.

Remi rushed to her hotel room door, ready to go down the hall and inform Daniel they needed to go to Denmark, no matter what the budget people at the FBI said.

Then she paused, remembering the scene at the hospital. When they had returned to the hotel, Daniel had gone off to a local kebab shop for dinner, no doubt knowing she wouldn't follow. She had gone to a proper restaurant instead. They hadn't spoken for a couple of hours.

Maybe going to his room would be awkward. It certainly would feel so for her, dressed as she was in her pajamas. Plus he might still be talking to Veronica.

She decided to call instead. Whatever awkwardness they might feel toward each other at the moment, they had to work around it. The answer to the case might be in Copenhagen.

Remi grabbed her phone, brought up his number, and stopped her finger just before touching the dial button. No, she'd send him a text instead. That would be easier for both of them. This was urgent, so if he didn't reply in ten minutes, she'd go over.

Yes, she promised herself. *Ten minutes and not a second longer.*

She sent a text explaining what she had discovered and the urgency of the situation, then paced. She should really go over. She was being silly. Daniel was a professional, and she had discovered a break in the case. Not going over was putting her feelings before the job.

Feelings? What feelings?

You have a job to do.

Her phone buzzed. A text from Daniel.

"Sounds like a good lead. I'll get to work on travel arrangements. It's going to be hard convincing them, though. The FBI is starting to get cheap."

And nothing else. Remi stared at her phone for a long time, disappointed. No more messages came.

CHAPTER NINETEEN

Remi felt a profound sense of relief to finally be in Copenhagen. There were no direct flights from Ljubljana, so they had to transfer through Frankfurt and only made it to the campus of the University of Copenhagen in the late afternoon.

The trip had been an uncomfortable one, with Daniel barely speaking to her. Instead he had checked his phone as obsessively as one of her undergraduate students.

Checking for texts from Veronica? Probably. He kept the screen turned away from her and replied to several messages. Remi delved into Sergio Ramon-Diaz's journal, trying to concentrate on teasing out more clues and ignoring the drama going on in the seat next to hers.

The more she read the journal, with the aid of a Spanish-English dictionary she grabbed at an airport bookshop, the more she grew convinced that Ramon-Diaz had learned much of what he knew from other people, most probably "V.C.". Entire sections of the journal gave the impression of having been copied from other sources. Some of these had been named. Others were marked "personal conversation." The latter tended to be longer entries and never had notations in blue ink. That suggested that V.C., presumably Viggo Christensen, had been the person Ramon-Diaz had spoken to. There would have been no need to correct or add to information he had provided the Spanish collector with.

Now they strolled through the open, leafy campus of the University of Copenhagen, a sharp autumn chill in the northern air. Imposing nineteenth-century stone buildings lined grassy quads, and above them soared the graceful towers of a couple of old churches. They passed laughing blonde students, many in couples, their bright blue eyes showing the optimism and promise of youth.

Remi suddenly felt old. Here she was approaching middle age having tossed aside a successful career to go into a terrifying and often unfruitful new job with nothing to go home to except memories of her ex-lover and the academic journals she no longer contributed to.

For a moment she doubted her decision to join the FBI. The exhausting hunts, the danger, the complications with her partner …

… and then she remembered Grayson. And Brentford. And Ramon-Diaz. All scholars and aesthetes like her. And all dead with their heads battered in by a hammer.

She had the knowledge and drive to find who did it. It fell to her to keep anyone else from getting hurt.

A heavy burden of responsibility, and yet a rewarding one. Looking back on her life, she realized that while she had always been a giving person with her friends and the brighter among her students, her life had been an essentially selfish one. She had chased after her own ambitions and her own need to satisfy her curiosity. She had never volunteered for charities like Cyril, or fought crime like Daniel.

Now that had all changed. Now she was useful.

Old? How could she feel old when she had a life like this?

"What are you smiling about?" Daniel asked.

"Um, nothing. The department is that building over there."

They had called ahead to the administration office to find out Viggo Christensen's schedule, and knew he would be finishing up a class in the next couple of minutes. They had decided to arrive unannounced to catch him off guard.

Not that Remi thought Christensen was the murderer. While they hadn't yet gotten his travel information, it didn't make much sense for the killer to help one of his victims to figure out the mechanism if what he really wanted was to keep the mechanism for himself. No, Christensen was more valuable for what insight he could give as what Ramon-Diaz had been thinking and perhaps who else he had spoken to about the device.

They came to the Classics building, an ornate stone edifice with heavy bronze doors flanked by imitation Roman statues of Diana. Passing through, they took a minute to find Christensen's lecture hall. Class was just getting out as they arrived.

About twenty students filed out, their books tucked under their arms and serious looks on their faces. Once again Remi felt a tug of nostalgia. European students were so much more focused than American students. It had been a pleasure to teach them.

As the last student left the class, they could see inside. A tall, slim man with thinning blonde hair that had not yet turned to gray was gathering his books in a leather satchel. He wore a dark brown suit, a green tie that didn't really match, and dress shoes. On the blackboard behind him was a lengthy text in Ancient Greek. Remi tried to figure out if this was the same handwriting as she had seen in the notebook. It was hard to tell. People wrote differently when writing on a blackboard.

The text was a quote from Xenophon. Remi read it out loud, translating to English, "You are well aware that it is not numbers or strength that bring the victories in war. No, it is when one side goes against the enemy with the gods' gift of a stronger morale that their adversaries, as a rule, cannot withstand them."

Viggo looked up, his blue eyes widening with surprise. While they hadn't seen each other in a year, and didn't actually know each other that well, he recognized her instantly. He hurried across the room.

"Remi Laurent? You didn't tell me you'd be here. Good to see you!"

This was said in his fluent French. When he noticed Daniel, he switched to English, extending a hand.

"Professor Viggo Christensen. Classics."

Daniel made that tight little smile he always got when he was about to spring a surprise on a suspect or suspicious witness. "Daniel Walker. FBI."

Viggo blinked. "FBI?"

Remi studied him. Most people would have assumed Daniel was joking, but the pale Dane had grown a bit paler, and had unconsciously taken a step back.

She didn't need any training to see that Viggo was a little worried about an FBI agent coming to call. Remi decided on a second test.

Remi pulled out her ID and held it up. "I'm with the FBI now too."

Viggo let out a little laugh and made an exaggerated grin. "Is this a joke?"

From the sound of his voice, he knew it wasn't.

"We'd like to ask you some questions about Sergio Ramon-Diaz," Daniel said. "I believe you know him."

A moment's hesitation. "Yes. He's an art collector in Spain. Remi, have you really left academia?"

"Let's stick to the topic, Professor Christensen," Daniel said before Remi could reply. "Could you describe the nature of your relationship with Mr. Ramon-Diaz?"

"Certainly. Let's go to my office, shall we?"

Before Daniel could answer, Christensen turned away and walked back to the front of the lecture hall to retrieve his satchel. There was no other exit than the one they stood by, so neither FBI agent made a move to stop him. When he returned, he gave them an uncertain smile and motioned for them to follow.

Remi walked by her colleague's side, Daniel walking behind. Remi noticed he walked directly behind Professor Christensen, out of his sight, a method she had learned both intimidated the witness and also made it easy to grab him if he tried to bolt.

Remi didn't think Christensen would make a run for it, although he did seem strangely nervous.

He also seemed loathe to talk. As they walked, he greeted everyone he passed, effectively stopping his conversation with the two FBI agents. Remi bided her time. So did Daniel, although she could practically feel him simmering with impatience. If they had been in private, Daniel would have probably grabbed the professor by the lapels and shook him until he revealed everything he knew.

They got to his office, a spacious corner room with a window overlooking the quad, the view mostly blocked by a large oak tree. The slanting sunlight shining though the leaves cast a greenish, under-the-sea tone to the office until Christensen switched on a light. A bookshelf was stuffed with volumes almost entirely in Ancient Greek. His desk was a mess of term papers. Once again Remi got hit with nostalgia. Not so long ago, this had been her life, not running around the world chasing killers.

Christensen sat behind the desk and gave them a flat smile. There was only one other chair in the room. Daniel gestured for her to take it. Remi decided to remain standing. It might give them a psychological advantage.

So would closing the door. She closed it. It felt surreal to be treating one of her own colleagues this way.

"So explain your relationship with Señor Ramon-Diaz," she said, repeating the question he had avoided for the past five minutes.

Professor Christensen gave a little shrug that struck her as overly casual. "He came to me for help. He was researching an early Greek clockwork device similar to the Antikythera mechanism. He visited me here in Copenhagen after he got in touch."

"Did he email you?" Remi asked. The Spanish police had already checked the victim's emails and there hadn't been any to Christensen. Sad to say, she hoped to catch him in a lie. She hated that she was doing this to a fellow academic. This was a serious case, however.

"No, he telephoned. He's quite an elderly gentleman and doesn't feel comfortable with modern technology. Odd considering his fascination with ancient technology."

He's talking about Ramon-Diaz in the present tense. Maybe he doesn't know he's dead.

That made sense. The murder only made the local news in Malaga, something the Danish scholar would be unlikely to read, and Ramon-Diaz had been a bit of a recluse, so they probably didn't have any mutual acquaintances.

"So tell us more about this clockwork device," Daniel said.

"It's actually a musical instrument. Various gears can be set to give tension to a spring that then strikes a series of tubes of a different length, making them ring out. Each tube gives a different note, and the level of tension to the spring changes the volume of the note."

"Why would someone use gears for that?" Daniel asked, even though he knew. He obviously wanted to see how forthcoming Christensen would be.

He turned out to be more forthcoming that Remi expected.

"The gears act as a dial where a specific strength and note can be set. It was intended as a healing instrument. One obscure branch of ancient Greek mysticism believed the music of the spheres dictated an individual's health, so the tones of the universe were intimately related to astrology and the body. These tones could be reproduced, and then focused on afflicted parts of the body to encourage healing. Ramon-Diaz believes that it might actually work."

Remi noted with surprise that this was said without a trace of irony.

"What do you think?" she asked.

He leaned forward, resting his hands on the table. "I find the whole subject fascinating. I've come across a few inscriptions related to the device. None of them published. As with your Medieval studies, the majority of Ancient Greek inscriptions have never seen print. There are simply too many. I've also looked at some papyrus from the Ptolemaic period. I had a wonderful and very fruitful visit to the National

Museum in Cairo a few years ago where I read some of their papyri, and discovered a lengthy treatise on just this subject."

"Did it mention the device?" Remi asked.

"Not as such, but it did provide a great deal of information on the concept of the music of the spheres and how it could be used in healing. It also included some of the incantations you would use, prayers to the Greek gods. Being a text from the period of Egyptian history when the country was under Greek rule, they incorporated Egyptian deities as well, especially Sekhmet and Osiris. In the spells included in the papyrus, they would strike a series of thin glass tubes in order to focus the musical tones on the afflicted part of the body. They had different sized and shaped tubes for different maladies."

"So the device used a glass tube!" Remi blurted. "Just as I thought, the gears would be set for a particular sickness, and strike the tubes to give off the right tone!"

As soon as she said it, Remi know she had revealed too much. Christensen was the one who was supposed to give up information, not her.

The Danish scholar only smiled. "I see you've done your research."

Daniel cut in. "Did Mr. Ramon-Diaz show you the piece of the device that he had acquired?"

"No. He didn't want to travel with it because it was so fragile. He showed me photos, though. Fascinating. He also had some photos of other pieces of the device from before restoration."

Those would be the original excavation photos in his journal, Remi thought.

"Did he mention where he got this piece?" Remi asked.

Christensen seemed to stiffen. "He said he bought it from an antiquities dealer. I don't recall him mentioning the name."

"Do you think he acquired it legally?"

"I don't see why he wouldn't have."

Remi was unconvinced. "Did he mention where the other three pieces are?"

"No. He's most anxious to acquire them. He's dying, the poor man, and he thinks the device can cure him. It's his last hope. May I ask why you're asking me all this? Did he buy the piece illegally?"

Daniel decided to drop his bomb. "Mr. Ramon-Diaz got murdered last week."

Christensen sat up, expressing what Remi felt was genuine shock. "What?"

"Someone broke into his house, or was invited in, and bludgeoned him to death with a hammer. The piece is now missing."

"My God. This is terrible! Wait, you don't think I did it, do you?"

"We don't have a named suspect as of now," Remi said, not answering his question and thus turning the screws a bit more. "We're more interested in your expertise on the device itself. You seem to know more about it than anyone."

"My God … murdered," Christensen whispered, lowering his gaze and shaking his head. After a moment he got a hold of himself. "I do know more about this device than anyone I know of. This has been a major thread of sideline research for quite some time now. I haven't published because I need more material. Something solid. Only once I have that can I submit my paper. Just wait until you read it. It's explosive! I can't publish before I have that proof, though. If you don't mind my saying, Remi, I didn't want to be treated like you have for your cryptex research."

Remi grimaced. She had endured a fair amount of mockery for her decade-long hunt. Most academics didn't think the cryptex was real until it turned up in a murder investigation, the very same investigation that led her to join the FBI. Researchers were very sensitive to their reputation, as it could affect collaboration opportunities, grant application, and publication.

The common expression in academia was that you had to "publish or perish." In reality, it was "be accepted or perish." She had only survived because of her groundbreaking research on medieval codes and hidden messages in illuminated manuscripts. If she had focused entirely on the cryptex, she would have been teaching night school for seniors at a community college.

Remi and Daniel exchanged glances. They seemed to have hit another dead end. Christensen, while acting strangely nervous, had been cooperative, but he didn't have anything to offer them that wasn't in the Spaniard's journal.

Remi made a move toward the door.

"If you come across any more information, you know how to get in touch with me," Remi said.

Christensen rose. "I'm so sorry to hear about Señor Ramon-Diaz. What a horrible thing to do to such an educated gentleman. At least he's no longer suffering. Poor man."

He moved around the desk.

"We'll see ourselves out," Daniel said.

They shook hands and the two FBI agents left the office.

"What do you think?" Remi asked in a low voice as they walked down the hall.

"I think he's hiding something. My gut says he's not the killer, though."

"I agree on both counts." Remi felt good to have perceived the same thing as the more experienced agent. She also felt relief that they had returned to a professional footing. While she couldn't deny she had developed feelings for him, it was all far too confusing when they were in the middle of an investigation.

"I contacted the Danish police to check on his travel history," Daniel said. "I haven't heard back yet. Since we're here, let's go to the administration building and see if he's taken a vacation or leave of absence lately."

"All right."

They walked in silence for a time, something niggling at the back of Remi's mind. Something the Danish scholar had said. No, not what he said, but the *way* he said it.

I haven't published because I need more material. Something solid. Only once I have that can I submit my paper. Just wait until you read it.

He had made it sound like the paper was already finished and that it would be published soon. She had gotten the impression that the proof he sought was almost in his reach.

What had Horvat said? That someone knew where the fourth piece was.

Remi stopped in the hallway, making a student walking behind her bump into her, mumble an irritated apology that expressed just whose fault it was, and circle around.

"He knows where the last piece is! I'm sure of it!"

CHAPTER TWENTY

If there was one thing Daniel had learned from this fascinating, frustrating woman, was that he should trust her instincts.

Daniel had suspected the guy was hiding something too. He had figured Christensen knew Ramon-Diaz's artifact had been stolen and was worried about covering his ass in front of the feds. But the possibility that he knew the location of the fourth piece was far juicier.

Made sense too. He was the world's expert on this obscure topic, perhaps the only expert now that Ramon-Diaz was dead. While Christensen said he had only made passing references to it in his work, anyone trawling through the literature for information on musical healing in the ancient Greek world would have come across these references and guessed his interest. The Spaniard might not have been the only person to consult him.

They rushed back to Viggo Christensen's office, only to find it locked, the light behind the frosted glass window off.

"Damn it!" Daniel said.

Christensen hadn't passed them, so they ran the other way down the hallway, making it to a broad set of stairs leading to the ground floor. They hurried down these, but caught no sight of the professor.

"Where could he have gone?" Remi asked.

"I don't know, but he's obviously avoiding us. He bolted the instant we were out of his office."

They ended up outside. Daniel scanned the quad, but didn't see him.

He snapped his fingers. "The parking lot! It's not far from here."

Because they didn't have an active case in Denmark, they hadn't been picked up by the local police and had rented a car at the airport. Daniel had no idea if the visitor parking lot was the same as the staff parking lot, or indeed if there was more than one parking lot for this university. They'd have to chance it.

They ran for the parking lot, hoping to catch a glimpse of Christensen.

They didn't spot him until they almost got to their rental car, when they saw him in a little Nissan pulling out of the lot.

"There he is!" Remi said a moment after Daniel saw him.

"Do you think he noticed us?" Daniel asked as he unlocked their rental.

"I don't know, but he certainly looked like he was in a hurry."

Daniel started the engine and pulled out, nearly clipping another car coming down the lane. He ignored a shouted bit of Danish he presumed were swear words, got into gear, and hit the gas.

He pulled onto the street just as Christensen ran a yellow light half a block away.

Daniel put on speed, cursing the underpowered vehicle the rental agency had given them. The light turned red well before they made it to the intersection.

"Hold on!"

Daniel swerved around a car cutting across their path, then swerved the other direction to avoid a bus. Remi screamed. Daniel might have screamed too but he was too busy trying not to get killed to check if he was being unmanly or not.

To a symphony of blaring horns, they made it through the intersection in one piece and sped down the street. Christensen was up ahead gaining speed.

Gaining a lot of speed.

If the professor hadn't noticed them in the parking lot, he sure had noticed them now.

Christensen was running away from the law, and that made him guilty.

Daniel floored it, then gritted his teeth in frustration to see Christensen's superior model pulling ahead.

They sped along a city street, both vehicles weaving between moderate late afternoon traffic. Cars were parked along both sides of the road, hemming them in. Daniel kept a sharp eye out for pedestrians. While he wanted to catch the guy, he didn't want to run over some clueless idiot walking across a pedestrian crosswalk while looking at their phone and not the world around them.

Two blocks later, that's exactly what happened to Christensen.

A teenage boy walked out onto a crosswalk, staring at his phone and assuming any vehicles would obey traffic regulations and stop for him.

Every vehicle did except for Christensen. He was going too fast to stop.

The professor slammed on his breaks, the squealing of tires on pavement loud even in a closed car half a block behind, and swerved to the right.

He almost made it. His right tires hit the curb and the entire car tilted. For a horrible moment Daniel, braking hard to avoid hitting the kid too, thought Christensen would flip over, but at the last moment the car righted itself.

But not enough. Christensen had lost control. He swerved, nearly went into the oncoming traffic on the other side of the road, and overcompensated to avoid them.

He ended up too far back on his side of the road and clipped a parked police car, sharing off the paint all along one side and smashing the sideview mirror.

Daniel laughed. He had a brief glimpse of two police officers rushing out of a shop toward their damaged vehicle and then honed in on Christensen. The guy was so rattled that he had slowed down enough for Daniel to overtake him.

Daniel got in the lane beside Christensen just as they blew a yellow light. A couple of slow cars ahead made them reduce their own speed, and that gave Daniel the opportunity to sideswipe Christensen's car.

He didn't do it hard, just enough to spook him.

Christensen, rattled from nearly running over that kid, got plenty spooked.

Spooked enough to immediately pull over, rear-ending a parked van in the process.

Daniel screeched to a stop and leapt out. Sprinting for Christensen, Remi just behind him, he got to the car before the professor could react.

As soon as he saw Christensen, he realized he hadn't needed to rush. The guy sat behind the wheel, his face in his hands and trembling all over.

You're not the murderer, are you? Someone who can kill three men with a hammer wouldn't react like this. But you know something. Oh yes, you know something, and I'm going to find out what it is.

Daniel wrenched the door open, unclipped Christensen's seatbelt, and hauled him out. He got a good grip on both lapels, gave him a good shake, then slammed him into the side of the car. Christensen looked terrified.

"Don't hurt him!" Remi cried.

"I'll hurt him if I want to hurt him," Daniel growled, although he didn't actually mean it. Christensen sure looked like he believed him, though. "Why were you running? What do you know about the murders."

"I … I … "

Before Christensen could formulate an answer, there was a shout in Danish to their right.

Daniel turned and saw the two police officers standing a few yards away, guns leveled.

"Whoops."

* * *

Two hours later, after giving their statements to the police, having their IDs checked, and a call to the United States to verify their claim, Daniel and Remi were finally allowed to question Christensen.

It felt nice to be free of the handcuffs, Daniel thought. He had put them on so many people and had never realize how uncomfortable they were.

While things were looking up, Daniel still had one worry—he hadn't informed the rental agency about the damage to their car. At least he had taken out accident insurance. He wasn't sure that covered driving suspects off the road, though. Probably not.

The bean counters at Resource Allocation were going to freak when they heard about that little stunt.

He'd deal with it later. First he wanted to grill Christensen, now that he wasn't going to jail himself. Maybe if he solved this case he wouldn't get stuck in some desk job in the FBI basement.

He and Remi went into the interrogation room with a young Danish officer whose name he didn't bother to learn. Daniel had hopped countries so many times in the past week that he had lost track of all the local officials he had had to deal with.

Danish interrogation rooms looked much like interrogation rooms anywhere else, with no furnishings other than a table and chairs, and a large one-way mirror on one wall. The only difference this time was the presence of a lawyer sitting next to Christensen.

The lawyer was a gaunt older man with a stony face who looked like he knew what he was doing.

Damn, Daniel thought as soon as he saw him. *I hate defense attorneys who know what they're doing.*

"We will conduct this inquiry in English for the sake of our foreign guests," the lawyer said as they stepped into the room.

Daniel disliked the sarcasm about "foreign guests" and the way the lawyer seemed to think he was in charge, but it wasn't like they could follow a line of questioning conducted in Danish.

They sat. The police officer started a recording and ran through the relevant information in Danish, then repeated it in near-perfect English. Daniel studied Christensen. He sat, slumped and resentful, glowering at his former colleague. Remi looked seriously embarrassed. Daniel pitied her. This was the first time they had hauled in someone she actually knew.

He turned his focus on Christensen. He certainly didn't pity this guy.

"So where were you going?" Daniel asked.

The professor and his lawyer traded a glance, then Christensen turned to them and in what sounded like a prepared statement said,

"I was heading to Sweden to see a researcher regarding the musical healing device. Like Señor Ramon-Diaz, he is a private collector who has been researching the mechanism and he asked me for help. He had read some of my articles and knew of my interest in the subject. I've written about it in several journal articles but until the excavation in Greece, I never had proof that the Greeks actually put their theory into practice with a clockwork mechanism. When you mentioned that Ramon-Diaz had been murdered, I feared for his life too and decided to see him."

"Why didn't you just call instead of sneaking out?"

"He suffers from paranoia. He believes all mobile phones are monitoring devices and that all landlines are tapped. The One World government follows all phone conversations. Or was it the Freemasons? I can't remember. In any case, is impossible to contact him in that manner. He only accepts letters, and that has to come to a post office box he rented out under a false name. Even then, he prefers that you write in Latin or Ancient Greek."

"Does this man have a name?" the police officer asked.

"Oskar Sverdrup. He lives in Gamla Uppsala."

"That's in Sweden?" Daniel asked.

"Yes."

"And how the hell did you plan to drive there? Isn't the North Sea in the way?"

Christensen smiled. The lawyer explained, "There's a bridge."

Daniel flushed. He'd never spent any time in Scandinavia. His mother, in her perpetual tours of Europe, had preferred more Mediterranean climates.

Eager to regain the advantage, Daniel said, "Why not just phone the Swedish authorities? And why didn't you tell us about this guy?"

Christensen looked at his attorney and then said, "Given his mental condition, I thought having the police show up at his house would be damaging to his emotional state. He trusts me. I would have been able to get him to a safe place. I didn't tell you for the same reason. You would have gone in there like you came at me, all questions and suspicions. He would not react well to that. It might even lead him to have a breakdown I ask that you please consider this when you go see him."

"That still doesn't explain why you ran from us."

"I didn't know it was you. I saw I was being followed, and sped up to see if my suspicions were correct. When the car following me ran a red light and nearly caused an accident, I became as paranoid as Oskar Sverdrup. I thought the killer was chasing me."

Daniel wasn't convinced. They had gotten close behind him, and he could have probably seen it was them in the car. And why not stop next to the police car they had passed and asked for help?

No, this guy was handing them a line.

Before he could reply, Remi cut in. "Does this Swedish researcher have a piece of the device?"

Christensen paused, his features showing an internal struggle, and then he gave a curt little nod as if he had come to a decision.

"Yes he does. Sverdrup bought it on the black market from a dealer in the Balkans. He—"

His lawyer interrupted him, saying something quick and cautionary in Danish. While Daniel didn't understand the words, he had heard the tone a million times. The suspect had gone too far and the lawyer was trying to reel him in before he incriminated himself.

Christensen said something back, and there was a brief, hushed argument as they hunched close to each other, shooting looks at the Danish policeman, who was the only other person in the room who understood what they were saying, assuming he could hear it. Even Remi's languages skills couldn't help Daniel here.

The argument grew increasingly heated, the volume going up until the policeman could hear every word. Like a pro, he sat there passively, allowing this free information to come to him.

With a final, dismissive gesture, Christensen turned away from his attorney and faced Remi. The attorney threw up his hands and looked like he wanted to leave.

"I'm sorry, Remi, but I wanted to protect you. That's why I didn't tell you about Sverdrup. He's absolutely mad, and I think … I think he killed Ramon-Diaz. I didn't think he'd be capable of such a thing, but now that Ramon-Diaz is dead, it must have been him."

"Why do you think that?" Remi asked.

"His father has Alzheimer's. The poor man has been in a home for years, completely unable to communicate with others or take care of himself. Sverdrup thinks the device can cure him, and he's determined to get all the pieces. He's been following the trail for years, ever since his father began to decline. Sverdrup knows as much about it as I do. And he … " Christensen hung his head. " … he knew about Ramon-Diaz having a piece of the device."

"How did he know that?" Daniel asked.

"I told him. I didn't think anything of it. I-I thought they could collaborate. But when you told me Ramon-Diaz had been killed, I knew it must be him. He's so unstable, flies into rages if he doesn't get what he wants. He has cut himself off from all but the most necessary human contact. He only tolerates me because I can help him. He's dangerous, Remi. Be very careful with him."

"If he's so dangerous," Daniel growled, "and you think he's the killer, why were you driving to Sweden to tell him about us?"

Christensen grimaced. His lawyer started to say something but the professor cut him off with a quick gesture.

"I … I wanted proof for my theory. I've been tracking this so long, having to keep most of what I suspected to myself. It's a lifetime of research. If I could prove it true, it would vindicate all the sacrifices I've made in pursuit of this thing." His eyes grew wide, eager. "I would be proven *right*. Professor Laurent knows what I'm talking about. Just like her, I've only been able to put snippets of information into my publications, hints and oblique references, because academia is too closed-minded to believe the things I want to tell the world. If I could only get proof … well … that would be worth the risk."

Daniel and Remi exchanged glances. He could tell from her expression that she believed her former colleague. Daniel was only partially convinced. While Christensen could very well be lying to cover himself, they had found no evidence that he had traveled outside of Denmark recently. The local police had searched of his home and found no pieces of the artifact.

But what he really so obsessed that he would offer himself up to the killer just to prove himself right?

Quite possibly. Remi has come close to doing the same thing with the Cryptex Killer. Oh, she explained that away as humoring the madman, stringing him along until help came, but Daniel knew that was only part of the truth. She wanted to know what the cryptex contained every bit as much as that psychopath.

And Christensen? Even if he was guilty and had the artifact hidden somewhere, he remained charged with reckless endangerment, interfering with a police investigation, and aiding and abetting antiquities smuggling. While he would probably be released on bond pending the trial, the law here would keep a close eye on him.

Damn, another country, another reclusive weirdo. The question is, will he be the killer or just another victim?

CHAPTER TWENTY ONE

One more piece. He needed only one more piece.

So close, and yet so frustratingly far.

Because he knew who owned it, but he didn't know where the bastard lived.

He sat in a café in Gamla Uppsala, "Old Uppsala" in Sweden, suppressing a jetlagged yawn and sipping his third cup of coffee. In front of him was a laptop with a historical article he was writing on Ancient Greek musical instruments.

Well, pretending to write, because he spent more time looking out the window than he did working on the paper.

For on the other side of the street stood the local post office, and inside that post office was where the post office boxes were.

Otto Sverdrup may have never revealed his home address, or indeed what he looked like or even his approximate age, but he did check his mail daily.

That was obvious by how quickly he would respond to letters.

Under a false name from his own P.O. box in the States, he had been corresponding with him for several months.

Sverdrup was a recluse, but he suspected that the man was not a recluse by choice. His long, friendly letters that ranged across many more topics than just his and Sverdrup's shared obsession spoke of a lonely man eager to reach out.

So he'd sit here in this cafe, ordering one coffee after another, and more of those tasty pastries they made, and wait for Sverdrup to show himself. He'd been here since just before nine, when the post office opened, and would stay until it closed at seven at night if he had to.

And how would he know Sverdrup from all the other Swedish men going in and out? Because he had Fedexed a large, distinctive green box the day before, and his delivery code said it had made it to the post office but had not yet been picked up. When he saw a man leave the building with that green box, he'd know he'd almost have the last piece of the Peloponnese mechanism in his grasp.

But why the hell was Sverdrup taking so damn long?

He shot a nervous glance at the beautiful young woman behind the counter. He'd been here hours already. While she hadn't made a mention of the fact, he had stayed far longer than anyone else in the café, even longer than those pensioners had played three games of chess in a row before finally strolling off somewhere else. She must have noticed him still hanging around.

Whatever she thought of this middle-aged foreigner taking up space in the café, she didn't complain. He kept buying things, after all.

He gave her another glance. Pretty. Pale Nordic skin, crystal blue eyes, and hair of such a light blonde it looked almost white. It had been a long time since he had desired or even looked at a woman. His wife's slow, agonizing death seemed to have destroyed his sexual urges.

During her long sickness and unstoppable decline, he had taken a leave of absence from the university and tended to her night and day. Their insurance didn't cover fulltime care until the very end. Acting as caregiver had left him physically and emotionally drained, and by the time she died he had no emotions left to feel.

The man that returned to the lecture hall and lab was a husk of the man everyone had known before.

His colleagues and students had all been kind. Patient. They had tried to be understanding, although no one who hadn't been through such torture could possibly understand.

Their kindness, patience, and understanding began to fray pretty quickly. He was short with everyone, careless in his work, distracted and late to meetings. If anyone tried to gently point out these failings, he'd fly into a rage, screeching at them for not understanding what he'd been through.

For four months, a whole academic term, people tolerated this periodic abuse. Then the dean pulled him in, all sympathy and soft words, and told him he should take a leave of absence, "to get some perspective."

Perspective? Perspective on losing his the most wonderful woman in the world to the ravages of cancer? Before he knew what he was doing, he picked up a heavy paperweight from the dean's desk and brought it down on the idiot's head. That would give him some damn perspective!

The paperweight hit the dean's temple with a satisfying crack. A beautiful sound, and the jarring impact gave him a thrill he had never known. The dean fell to the side with a groan, and he raised the paperweight again, ready to strike.

He caught himself. With an effort that frightened him with its difficulty, he put the paperweight down and stammered out an apology. The secretary rushed in, alerted by the sound, and screamed.

It was then that he knew the rest of his life, not just his marriage, was well and truly over.

The dean did not press charges, although of course he got fired and barred from ever coming back on campus. Fine by him. He didn't need those fools, for he had been quietly doing some research on the side, and had discovered that a certain stolen artifact had a lot more value that its age.

Some research that showed that the artifact, which he had never had time to properly examine, was the one thing that could have saved her.

Too late! She was beyond helping now. Tears formed in his eyes, which he quickly brushed away. He glanced around. No one seemed to have noticed. Everyone was busy texting or chatting. The pretty girl behind the counter was helping a customer. He remained unnoticed. Alone.

He stared gloomily out the window, returning to his vigil.

A short, squat man hurried out of the post office, carrying the large green package.

Springing out of his seat, he hurried to put his laptop in his bag and walked with a quick step out of the café.

"Time to get this done," he muttered.

Oskar Sverdrup had already made it half a block down the street, walking with a remarkably fast gait for one so short and out of shape. As healthy as his pursuer was, he had to make an effort to keep up. As he did, he studied him.

Sverdrup looked to be in his early forties, with thinning blonde hair and a pudgy frame. From what little he knew, Sverdrup was a recluse living off an inheritance. Besides his research, food was probably his only pleasure. Despite this, his jerky stride took him down the sidewalk faster than anyone else in sight. Several times he overtook walkers and, with an air of impatience, passed around them. At one point, blocked by a young couple walking a toddler between them and blocking the sidewalk, Sverdrup stepped onto the street to make it past.

Social anxiety, the man following him realized. *Being out in public makes him afraid, and he's trying to get home as soon as he can.*

That could be useful.

Sverdrup led him on a long walk through the old part of town, where tidy stone homes from the eighteenth century or even earlier lined the streets. It was an overcast date, slate gray and cold. The decent weather Europe had enjoyed for the past couple of weeks was turning and winter looked like it would come early.

He followed Sverdrup out onto an open area, a path with grassy fields to either side. From here he could see the spires of the city's soaring cathedral in the distance, as well as the old castle on a nearby hill. Only a jogger and a couple of dog walkers remained in sight. This made him worry that the recluse might look over his shoulder and spot him, but it turned out he didn't need to fear. Sverdrup kept looking straight ahead, walking his stiff-legged, rapid stride, the green package clutched in his hands, eager to make it home.

They passed a small stone church that the man who hunted him had read dated back all the way to the 12th century. A cold stream ran behind it, the water gray and opaque. Local legend said it had been blessed by an early saint and had miraculous healing properties. Scattered in the field were several large slabs of stone, each with a flat face inscribed with runes. Beyond those rose three large mounds of earth in a row.

Long before Uppsala became Sweden's leading university town, this older village on its outskirts had been the seat of the Norse kings of Sweden and a center for pagan worship. When Christianity came to the north, the Church was quick to put up churches and forbid the old rites. They had not, however, dared to pull down the runestones or level the burial mounds of the great kings of yore. The northerners had a strong sense of pride and heritage, and while they now bowed their heads to God and not Odin, they would not entirely do away with old things.

He had to respect that. The past held more wisdom than most people realized. It even held the key to life itself.

The Swedes were wrong about that spring being able to heal. No, only the Peloponnese Mechanism could do that.

He staggered as the grief overcame him once more. The key to life, yes. The mechanism would give him that, but it would not bring back the dead.

Nothing could do that.

Still, he had to have it. Just holding such a thing would be a comfort, and a vindication. He'd show it to the world. Think how it would revolutionize medicine! It would save countless lives. The deaths of a few pathetic loners and antiquities thieves would be worth it. The world would forgive him, he was sure of it.

Oh, when he went public, perhaps with a demonstration on one of the surviving members of his wife's cancer support group, the police would arrest him and charge him with the murders. He had no doubt about that. But then as more of the devices were produced, and people became free of diseases they had suffered for years, the public outcry would set him free.

He smiled at the thought. His name and face everywhere … his old university naming a building after him … the Nobel Prize …

Oskar Sverdrup leaving the far side of the field and heading down a semi-rural road took him out of those pleasant thoughts. He wouldn't have any of that acclaim or validation unless he got that final piece.

The recluse continued his fast pace, visibly winded now and yet showing no sign of slowing down. He could hear the Swede's panting as he trailed him a hundred yard behind. Sverdrup didn't look back. He didn't even look to the left or right. He only focused at getting back home as quickly as possible.

Why does he even want the device? He doesn't look like he enjoys life.

They walked down the rural road, the village of Gamla Uppsala now behind them, and the newer city of Uppsala only visible in the distance as the cathedral spire, the castle on the hill, and a few tall modern buildings. To their left stretched an open field, to their right the last of the village's buildings. A few trees lined the road.

The man bit his lip. If Sverdrup turned around now, he'd know for sure he was being followed.

But he didn't. Sverdrup hurried on, making it to a row of three little stone houses. He went to the front door of one, set the package down, and pulled out a key.

As the key rattled in the lock, the man who followed him moved to the other side of the street to get out of Sverdrup's peripheral vision. He took a look around. No one in the houses. This might be the right … *damn!*

Directly across from Sverdrup's house, four woman stood chatting as their small children chased each other around and played with a little dog. No way he could come up on Sverdrup with these people around.

The yapping of the dog and the laughter of the kids seemed to mock him. So close, and now he would have to pass by and come back around later.

But he would come back. Tonight. When the kids were tucked in bed and their mothers were sitting in front of the television with their husbands. He knew the house now.

Sverdrup opened the door, carried the package in, and closed the door behind him.

The man who had sent him the package smiled. He had sent the recluse a stack of books on Ancient Greek music. Anonymously, of course.

You might as well have something enjoyable to read on your last night on Earth, Sverdrup.

CHAPTER TWENTY TWO

Remi couldn't believe what she had heard. Christensen had become so obsessed with finding the clockwork healing device that he was willing to give himself over to the killer? Insane! Who would do that?

The Classics professor had obviously become unbalanced, and she resented his comparing himself to her. While they had both worked in partial secret for years on their respective projects, Remi hadn't offered herself up as a lamb to the slaughter just to prove herself right.

She hoped Daniel didn't think she was like that. Despite his brusque manner and terrible eating habits, his opinion mattered to her.

How much did it matter? She didn't want to think about that. There were feelings there, on both sides, but those feelings were inappropriate for their professional situation. It had been bad enough having to hide her relationship with Cyril, the head of the history department at Georgetown where she had been visiting. The strain of that secret had been one of the things that had broken them. And having a relationship with a partner in a crime investigation would not only be unprofessional, it could be so distracting as to be dangerous.

Then there was Veronica. Strange how little Remi thought about her. She had only met her once and the first impression had not been a good one. Cold and aloof. She wasn't right for Daniel, Remi felt sure of that, not that it was any of her business.

Remember that. It's none of your business.

Daniel drove them along the Øresund Bridge, a long span of concrete and steel over the rough waters of the strait between Denmark and Sweden. The sun was behind them, peeking over puffy clouds as it set over the flat fields of Sjaelland, the island on which Copenhagen stood. Ahead they could see the coast of Sweden.

Daniel still drove the rental car he had damaged when stopping Viggo Christensen. While Remi wasn't sure if he was allowed to take it into Sweden, she felt certain he was supposed to report the damage to the rental agency as soon as possible. He had managed to convince the police in Copenhagen to "forget" to file a report for a few hours. He was good at that.

Her phone rang. It was the number of the central police station in Copenhagen.

"It's them," she told her partner. "Hopefully they've tracked down Oskar Sverdrup."

She answered. "Special Agent Remi Laurent."

Saying that still gave her a little thrill.

A man's voice came on in English. "Hello. This is Officer Guntarson. Is Special Agent Daniel Walker there?"

Remi frowned. *Yes, ask for the man.* "He's driving. Have you found the address we asked for?"

"We spoke with the police in Uppsala and they checked. There is no Oskar Sverdrup living in the city."

"What? But he has a post office box."

"They checked with the post office. Anyone hiring a post office box has to show identification and the post office keeps a photocopy. They checked this and the identification appears to be false. The address the person gave on the form does not exist."

Remi groaned. "Well, have them question the post office employees and see if they know him. Canvas the area."

"They're checking on that. Sverdrup is a common name, however. It might take some time."

Time is something we don't have.

Remi looked at the car's GPS. Uppsala was well up the east coast of Sweden and the screen informed her that they still had almost eight hours of driving. There had been no flights from Copenhagen to Uppsala until the next morning.

Remi had put the phone on speaker so Daniel could hear. He sped up.

Not that it would help. By the time they got there and tracked down Sverdrup, or whatever his real name was, he might be long gone.

Or he might be dead.

* * *

They arrived at Uppsala past midnight. The Swedish police had tracked down Oskar Sverdrup. It turned out he hadn't covered his tracks all that well. Oskar Sverdrup was his real name but the house wasn't registered under his name, it was registered under his mother's name. She had died the previous year and Sverdrup hadn't changed the paperwork. It appeared his trick at the post office was only to keep strangers from finding him. Postal workers said he got an inordinate amount of mail from all over the world, much of it was strange drawings on the envelopes.

That detail struck Remi as odd. While all the local witnesses the Uppsala police had spoken to said that Sverdrup was a recluse who no one knew hardly at all, he seemed to keep up a lively correspondence with a global network of people.

A group of similar minds, perhaps?

They'd soon see. She rubbed gritty eyes as they passed through the small northern city, floodlights illuminating a beautiful old cathedral and a giant castle on a hill. Remi had managed to doze on the way up here. Daniel had fueled his long drive with hamburgers and McDonald's coffee. Trust him to find a drive-through McDonald's in Sweden in the middle of the night.

Her phone buzzed. The Uppsala police. The Danish police had gotten them in touch and they had been giving updates ever since.

A woman's voice came on.

"Hello. This is Officer De Geer. Officer Bildt and I are still on stakeout."

Remi smiled at the American slang this Swedish officer used. Perhaps she had been inspired to join the force thanks to American crime movies.

Officer De Geer went on.

"Sverdrup has been in his house all night. We can see the entire house quite clearly and we are sure he hasn't left."

"Has anyone approached?"

"The house? No. There are several people across the lane having a star party."

"A what?"

"We have a local pensioner here, Starry Siebert we call him. He likes to bring a telescope out to a field across from Sverdrup's house, where it is very dark, and he shows people the stars and planets. He's been out there since about just after sunset. Many people have come and gone. No one has approached the house, though."

"Thank you. We're almost there."

Remi hung up.

"That gathering should keep away any prowlers," she said.

"Assuming anyone's coming after him," Daniel replied. "Glad we're almost there. That old man with stars in his eyes probably won't stay out there all night."

"If anyone tries to break in, Officers De Geer and Bildt can handle it."

"Never rely on anyone else unless you absolutely have to."

Remi blinked. That had been said without a trace of irony. Sometimes Daniel could be terribly antisocial. While he tried to hide it, that came out every now and then.

They checked the GPS and saw the rural lane right at the edge of the suburb of Gamla Uppsala was close.

"We'll park a couple of hundred yards down the road and walk under cover of darkness," Daniel said. "I want to get the lay of the land."

"Meters."

"Huh?"

"They use meters here. Here and everywhere else."

"Everywhere else but America, and the FBI is an American operation. We walk in yards."

"America isn't a country, it's a continent."

"America is an attitude. It's kicking dictator's asses and buying slushies at AM/PM mini malls. God bless America! Whohoo!" Daniel pumped his fist in the air.

Remi rolled her eyes.

"You just rolled your eyes, didn't you?" Daniel asked.

"How did you know that?" Remi asked, amazed.

"Because you always roll your eyes when I'm being patriotic."

"You're not being patriotic, you're being boorish," Remi said, nudging him.

"Want an Egg McMuffin? There's a couple left."

"Now you're just being annoying."

"To know me is to love me." Daniel's grin was clear in the faint streetlight.

Remi tensed. Daniel's grin vanished. She looked away. Daniel said nothing for the next couple of minutes until they came to a darkened lane and pulled over. The GPS told them Sverdrup's house stood just down the road. Remi sent a quick text to the Swedish officers telling them they had arrived.

"Let's go," Daniel said, his voice sounding strained.

The northern night air felt sharp with the chill of autumn. Remi buttoned up her coat, then quickly unbuttoned it again. She needed to keep it open in case she had to go for her gun.

They walked along a quiet rural lane with no streetlights and no moon. The clouds that had covered the country for most of the day had broken up and disappeared, revealing a sky full of stars. In the distance stood three houses, each with lights shining from behind their curtains. Remi could just make out the shadow of a car between themselves and the houses. Off to the left, opposite the houses, Remi spied a couple of faint red lights out in a darkened field.

She stopped.

"What's that?" she whispered. "Those red lights over there."

"That's the star party," Daniel whispered back. "They're using red light so they can adjust the telescope. You dial in declination and right ascension to look at whatever part of the sky you want. That's like latitude and longitude on earth. You need to be able to see the dials, though, and red light doesn't affect night vision."

Remi cocked her head, impressed. "How did you know all that?"

"I used to date an astronomer."

"Oh."

"Let's go."

They walked to the unmarked car. Just before they made it, a woman slipped out of the passenger side, hunkering low behind the car. Remi supposed that was so the people in the field wouldn't spot her, although in this darkness there seemed little risk of that.

Even so, Remi found herself automatically imitating her. So did Daniel. They ended up by the side of the car crouching with a Swedish policewoman they could barely see. Remi smiled. She sure found herself in odd situations these days.

"Hello, I am Officer De Geer. Officer Bildt is in the car," she said in English, motioning toward the car's invisible interior. "So far we haven't seen anyone come or go. We've made some discreet inquiries around the neighborhood and found that Sverdrup has been living in the same house most of his life. He inherited it from his parents, who both died recently. While there have never been any complaints about him, he is known in the area for avoiding people. We think he has a mental issue but he has no record of hospitalization. His parents were by all accounts quite normal."

"No criminal record?"

"None. But we did discover that he was gone for the past week."

"Gone?"

"Yes. He was spotted at the train station. Very unusual, since he never goes there or indeed anywhere other than the shops, and the people at the post office said he didn't come in for at least a week. That's unusual for him. He comes in every day without fail."

"A recluse who disappears for a week just when the murders took place?" Daniel whispered. "I think we have our man."

Remi nodded, before she realized how useless that motion was in the dark. "Do you have any record of where he went?"

"We're waiting for a court order. The ticket master says he paid in cash to go to Stockholm. From there he could take a train to anywhere in Europe, and if he paid cash the whole way, we wouldn't know where he went."

"Is he rich?" Daniel asked.

"Both his parents were successful professionals, a tax attorney and a radiologist. Plus he inherited the house. No siblings. So yes, he has independent means."

"Let's go," Remi said.

The male officer must have understood English as well because he slipped out of the passenger side door. They looked around for a moment and saw no one nearby, only the red lights bobbing like demon's eyes out in the field.

As they approached the line of houses, the male police officer cut through the space between Sverdrup's house and the neighboring home and disappeared into the shadows. The female officer slowed, allowing her partner to get into position to secure the back door.

They work well together, Remi thought. *Just like Daniel and I. I wonder if they feel ...*

Don't be stupid.

They came to the front door and Officer De Geer knocked.

An instant later it was flung open, and a short, portly man with thinning hair burst outside, face twisted in rage.

Remi went for her gun.

CHAPTER TWENTY THREE

Remi stopped herself from drawing her gun as she saw the man who had opened the door do nothing but scream in Swedish and wave his hands in the air.

Officer De Geer spoke in soothing tones, making calming gestures with her hands.

Remi had never studied the Scandinavian languages and had no idea what was being said, but from the man's gestures he seemed to be complaining about the star gazers in the field opposite.

The female officer continued to try and calm the man. Remi glanced over at Daniel and found he had taken a step back to get out of reach. Remi followed suit, cursing herself for not remembering this basic precaution.

Every encounter in every case was like a surprise quiz. Sometimes she got an A; other times she got a C.

She didn't want to think what would happen if she got an F.

Remi caught the officer using Sverdrup's name and immediately focused in more on his mannerisms. So this was the man they were after. While he didn't look all that physically fit, he was full of nervous energy and incandescent rage. She'd faced people like this before. They could be far, far, more dangerous than their appearance suggested.

After a minute, Officer De Geer managed to get Sverdrup calmed down enough for him to notice that the two people standing in the porch light behind the policewoman were not in uniform. He pointed to them and asked a question. Officer De Geer replied. Remi caught the word, "FBI."

Oskar Sverdrup stared at them a moment, his anger vanishing and replaced with blank curiosity.

He switched to English. "What are the FBI doing here?"

Remi stepped forward, although still keeping some distance between her and the suspect. She didn't want to take any chances, even with backup.

"We're here investigating the theft of some ancient Greek antiquities."

"Stolen antiquities? Well, I know nothing about it. Just get those stargazers out of the field. Their noise bothers everyone!"

Remi had barely heard them at all.

Sverdrup stepped back and tried to close the door.

Officer De Geer stuck her boot in the door and snapped out something in her own language. Sverdrup opened the door again, obviously astonished. He stared at each of his visitors in turn, and then mumbled in English, "Fine. Come in if you want to."

They entered a small entrance hallway with a heavy coat and raincoat on hooks and a pair of boots set beneath them. Remi noted fresh mud on the boots. Officer De Geer said something into a walkie talkie and got a short reply from her partner. Sverdrup looked at her curiously and then motioned for them to follow.

They ended up in a small living room. The heavy oak roof beam running along the ceiling and the large stone fireplace looked original. Remi realized this house was older than it looked on the outside, perhaps early 18th or even late 17th century.

While her historical eye was first caught by these details, they soon got distracted by the walls.

They were covered in hundreds of drawings.

The drawings were of every description, from simple sketches and collages to detailed landscapes or abstract paintings. Most were on simple printer paper or even lined pages torn from a notebook. Here and there she saw a few on the special paper artists used. There were even decorated envelopes, some with specially printed fake stamps next to the real ones. The drawings all seemed to be by different artists of a wide range of styles and abilities.

So this is what the postal workers were talking about.

Sverdrup shifted from one foot to another, obviously ill at ease.

"This is mail art," he said.

"What's mail art?" Daniel asked, staring at the pictures. They took up almost every available space from where the wall met the carpet all the way up to the ceiling. The only blank spots were around the fireplace, where a couple of logs crackled merrily.

Sverdrup shrugged. "Whatever you want it to be. You do any kind of art you feel like, and trade it with people through the post. I have correspondents all over the globe. I sketch nature scenes or historical buildings and send them to other mail artists, and they send me things in return. Every piece is unique. I've been doing it for almost twenty years now and have one of the largest collections in the world."

Remi tore her eyes away from the colorful walls and looked around the room. The furnishings were old and needed reupholstering. Used plates and cups littered the side tables and coffee table. Also on the coffee table sat a stack of books. A green box with a Fedex sticker sat open next to it.

The cover of the top book in the stack caught her eye.

Ancient Greek Religious Music, published by Harvard University Press.

She stepped over to the books and looked through them one by one. All were on the music of ancient Greece. Looking in the box, she saw more books on mythology and Greek medicine.

"Oh, that," Sverdrup said. "Another hobby of mine."

Daniel spotted the books too and edged around to get more behind Sverdrup. Officer De Geer remained at the doorway to the front hall, blocking it.

Sverdrup's eyes flicked from one to the other. His right hand began to twitch.

"I'm a historian too," Remi said, "specializing in Medieval history. Have you ever heard of the cryptex?"

"Vaguely," the Swede said with a dismissive wave that Remi found professionally insulting. "Some sort of conspiracy theory. Is that what this is about?"

"No. We're looking for stolen parts of the Peloponnese Mechanism."

Sverdrup blinked three times in rapid succession. His hand twitched more.

"Stolen artifacts? I have a small collection of antiquities but they are all registered as legal. I'm very careful about that."

"Could you show me?"

"All right. This way." He led them down a short hallway past a messy bedroom and to a small study.

The walls of the hallway were covered in mail art just like the living room. Remi casually glanced at all the colorful designs as she passed, until one in particular made her stop short with a gasp.

It was a drawing of a medallion, almost identical to the one Remi had found in the catacombs with various meandering lines leading to a central boss. Beside it was a photocopy of a modern map in German.

"What's this?" Remi asked, her voice coming out barely a whisper.

"That's by a pen friend of mine. He's interested in history too. It's a medieval medallion in his local museum. He figured out that the lines were actually the courses of streams and rivers flowing off a mountain in the Bavarian Alps."

Daniel came up beside her and pointed to the signature at the bottom corner of the drawing.

"Vater Vogel. Vater means 'father' in German," Daniel said. Remi shivered a little.

"Yes, he's a Catholic priest," Sverdrup said.

"What else do you know about this?" Remi asked.

"Not much. He's very proud of his discovery and said he is preparing an article about it. That was a couple of months ago. He sent me this drawing and the map. I think he's got it right. He promised to send me the article once it comes out."

"Can I … take a photo of this?" Remi asked.

Both Sverdrup and Officer De Geer stared at him curiously.

"Uh … all right," Sverdrup said.

Remi pulled out her phone and took several shots. Once she was done, she and Daniel stared at the drawing and map for a second longer, stunned.

Daniel recovered first. He shook himself as if waking up and turned to Sverdrup. "Show us your antiquities collection."

"This way."

Sverdrup passed through into a study, the police officer right behind him.

Remi stopped short in the doorway, overwhelmed for the second time in as many minutes, for there, on the wall, hung the completed Peloponnese Mechanism.

While she had only seen photos of the pieces when they had been fresh out of the ground on the original excavation, she knew this was the right device.

A circular brass plate had small lines along the circumference every millimeter or so. Ancient Greek inscriptions were inscribed just below these, naming various parts of the body. In larger letters further out on the edge of the plate were the labels “blood,” “yellow bile,” “black bile”, and “phlegm”. The four humors the ancient Greeks believed dictated the health or diseases of the body. These were marked by thicker lines that separated the back plate into four equal quarters.

Attached to the back plate was a complex system of interlocking gears that connected to a thin metal spring next to a cluster of glass tubes pointing outward.

Remi stared. Yes, this was exactly how it was supposed to fit together. Everything in Ramon-Diaz’s journal confirmed it.

Ramon-Diaz, one of the victims of the nervously twitching man who stood just a couple of paces from her.

One set of gears had not been restored. Trying to keep her voice steady, she pointed at them.

“Did you buy these?”

“Yes, from a dealer in Berlin. I have the paperwork here somewhere.”

Sverdrup moved to the desk and was about to open the drawer when Daniel cut him off. Remi’s partner gave him a hard look that made the recluse take a step back.

“Just stand over there and don’t make any sudden moves,” Daniel told him.

Daniel opened the drawer and found a mess of papers. He started shuffling through them and pulled out the one Sverdrup indicated.

He handed it over to Remi. She studied the papers as Officer De Geer looked over her shoulder.

“I don’t really read German but the stamps on this look correct,” she said. The Swedish officer nodded in agreement.

“You see? I’m not a thief.”

“Except we know that part of the device was stolen from an excavation in the Peloponnese several years ago,” Remi said in a flat voice. “So these papers are nothing but a clever fake. These other parts were stolen too.”

Officer De Geer pulled out a set of handcuffs and said something in Swedish. Remi didn’t know the words but knew she was reading him his rights.

Sverdrup started shaking all over, sputtering out words in Swedish. The officer replied and stepped forward. Sverdrup shouted and rushed forward, trying to push her to one side and make it to the door.

Remi drew her gun. Officer De Geer got Sverdrup in an armlock, tripped him and threw him face first to the floor. Within a couple of seconds she had her knee on the small of his back, his hands behind him, and was putting the cuffs on.

"Nicely done," Daniel said with a grin.

Glad that's over with, Remi thought, her hand straying to her pocket to caress the phone that stored those precious images of the medallion. *Now I can figure out what spot my medallion is pointing to, and get the next cryptex clue before anyone else.*

Assuming all this time chasing down this man hasn't given the competition a chance to grab it for themselves.

CHAPTER TWENTY FOUR

As Remi sat in Uppsala's main police station while Sverdrup got processed, she grew increasingly uneasy.

The device that she had carefully put in a padded evidence box lay open on her lap. Now that she had been able to study it for a time without the distraction of a murder suspect standing right next to her, she realized it was all wrong.

Or to be precise, it was mostly wrong.

The three gears that had been inexpertly cleaned and oiled were obviously original. The others, which in her initial shock she mistook for being original and expertly restored, were clearly modern replicas. She could see the machine tooling on the surfaces.

At first she thought that Sverdrup had used the stolen pieces as a model for creating a replica, but then realized that if he had done that, he wouldn't have used some original gears. Plus he didn't have a restoration workshop in his house like Ramon-Diaz, and police hadn't found the other missing pieces.

A closer look at device itself gave her further doubts. Some of the hash marks had inconsistent spaces between them, making the device imprecise, and she spotted a misspelling of one of the words. In addition, the network of gears didn't quite match those drawn in the Spanish notebook.

This was a modern replica, and not a particularly good one.

She walked across the open office of the police station to where Sverdrup sat with his head bowed, wrists handcuffed in front of him and one leg jerking up and down. At a desk next to him, an officer filled out a form about the new prisoner. Daniel stood to one side, arms crossed, staring at the unhappy man.

"Where did you get this?" Remi asked.

Sverdrup looked up. Remi saw tears in his eyes and felt a tug of sympathy.

As a recluse, the idea of jail must be terrifying.

"I-I tried to tell you. Ever since I bought those gears a few years ago I've been studying the device they came from. I read up on it all and talked to a bunch of experts. Then I had this reconstruction made with the original gears as part of it. Don't try to use it, though. The old gears are delicate and I've only used it a couple of times to make sure it works."

"Have you used it to heal yourself?" Remi asked.

Sverdrup looked at her as if she had said something stupid. "Huh? It doesn't work. It's magic. The Greeks thought it would heal people but of course you can't get rid of disease with sounds."

"The person who has been killing to get the pieces thinks it can."

Sverdrup's eyes widened. "Those people you accused me of killing, they all had other pieces?"

"Yes."

The man started trembling even more. "My God! How did he track them down? If he's got the others, then he's going to come after me. I need police protection!"

He turned to the officer at the desk and started shouting in Swedish. It took a minute for everyone to get him calmed down enough that Remi could question him again.

"Did the dealer in Berlin offer you any other pieces?"

"No. I asked, and he said this was the only one he had. I told him that if he ever found any more, to get in touch because I wanted them. I swear I didn't know it was stolen."

"So where did you go when you disappeared for a week?"

"I went to Stockholm to visit the antique stores, and then to Vienna and Prague to see some art shows. There was a premiere at the Kunsthistorisches Museum. I'm a member there and get in on a member's-only visit before the main exhibition opens. Fewer people that way. I'm a platinum member, which gets me an exclusive look. Only five other people were there when I was. That's the way to really enjoy art, not with a horde of people all crowding around you."

Sverdrup took a look around at the busy police station and shuddered.

"Why did you use cash at the Uppsala train station?"

"Why not?"

"Did you use a credit card for your further journeys?"

"I prefer cash."

Paranoid about companies selling his data, or trying to hide something?

"What did you do in Prague?"

"Have you ever walked through Prague at night?"

"Yes."

"It's beautiful. I get an Airbnb so I don't have to deal with anyone. I don't like hotels. Then I go out at about two in the morning. There's no one on the streets but they keep all the best buildings lit up. Beautiful. So peaceful."

What a lonely life you lead. You have no one.

"Do you have proof for any of this?"

"Sure. Let me get on the Airbnb site and show you. Plus I have my eticket for the exhibition."

A little groan behind her made her turn. Daniel had a defeated look on his face.

Remi felt the same. If Sverdrup was offering to show them proof, it could only be because that proof was solid. Daniel retrieved his laptop and allowed Sverdrup to access the sites he had mentioned.

Remi walked off. She knew what the result would be. Another dead end. Sverdrup wasn't their killer.

But the killer had to be close. This poor man owned the last piece. The killer was probably here in Uppsala right now. He might have even come to Sverdrup's old suburb and scouted out the house.

What if he saw us going in? Or the police car parked outside right now as the local police continue to search his house?

She hunted down Officer De Geer and explained the situation to her.

The policewoman gave a curt nod and said, "I'll pull out the officers searching the house and Officer Bildt and I will take the unmarked car back on stakeout. If anyone tried to break in, we'll catch them."

Remi smiled. This woman was a professional and a quick thinker. Too bad she lived in another country. Remi could learn a lot from her.

"Daniel and I would like to be on the stakeout too."

"I'll arrange it." The policewoman hesitated a second, and then asked, "Is it traditional in America to refer to your partner by their first name?"

Remi didn't speak for a second. Not only did the question embarrass her, but she didn't actually know the answer. It had never occurred to her to refer to Daniel as Special Agent Walker, like the assistant director did.

"It's … normal in the FBI."

Officer De Geer nodded and pulled out her phone. Remi turned away to keep the policewoman from seeing her blush.

* * *

The night was quiet. The clock glowing on the dashboard of the unmarked car parked with sight of Sverdrup's house read 3:45 AM. The stargazers had gone home hours ago.

Daniel and Remi sat in back while the two Swedes sat in front. No one had come down the lane for more than two hours, and Remi was getting the impression that the real killer had been scared off.

Still, they had to wait and see.

In the meantime, Remi had some following up to do. She had racked her brain as to who Horvat meant when he said someone else knew where the pieces were, Unfortunately a call to the Slovenian hospital had revealed that he remained unconscious and unable to speak. The doctors didn't think he'd be well enough for questioning for at least another couple of days.

Remi looked at the original report again, the one given to them by Assistant Director Ochiai. It included information about the original excavation. The dig director was a man named Tyler Ogden who was an assistant professor at UCLA. She and Daniel hadn't bothered to contact him because he had been cleared of theft all those years ago and their line of inquiry had driven them forward. Now that they were stuck, maybe Professor Ogden could give them some idea of who else might be an expert on this device, someone who the killer might have been in contact with.

Keeping her phone as dim as possible to make it less visible to anyone in the street, she looked up the faculty at UCLA. To her surprise, he wasn't listed. A Google search didn't find him at any other university either. In fact, it didn't reveal any activity at all for more than two years.

A photo of him on an excavation a few years ago revealed he was in his middle years, too young to have retired. Had he died? She couldn't find an obituary either.

"I'm calling UCLA," she told Daniel.

"On your cell phone? Resource Allocation is going to love that."

"What's Resource Allocation?" Officer Bildt asked from the front seat.

"The people who decide how much money we can spend on investigations," Daniel replied.

"Screw Resource Allocation," Officer Bildt said.

"Shut them down and use their budget for more investigations," Officer De Geer said.

Daniel grinned and jerked a thumb toward the front seat. "I like these two."

Remi smiled. "So do I."

Remi called the archaeology department at UCLA with the wicked hope that the call would cost a lot. It was nearly seven at night there. Remi wondered if anyone would pick up.

The phone rang, and rang.

Remi cursed under her breath and was about to hang up when someone picked up.

"Archaeology Department," a woman's voice said. "Professor Warren speaking."

Must be teaching a night class or running the lab. I'm lucky to get someone.

"Hello. I'm Professor Remi Laurent. I'm looking for Professor Tyler Ogden."

Pause. "I'm sorry, who were you looking for?"

"Professor Tyler Ogden."

"He … doesn't work here anymore." She sounded uncomfortable.

"Where does he work?"

"Nowhere, I hope."

The heat with which Professor Warren said this took Remi aback.

"Why do you say that?"

The professor countered with a question of her own. "How well do you know Professor Ogden?"

"Not at all. I had a research question."

"Ask someone else. The man has gone totally off the rails." Professor Warren said.

"It seems strange that a respected archaeologist and scholar would have such a break in personality."

Professor Warren paused, then said in a softer tone. "It's not entirely his fault. His wife had a long battle with cancer and died a few years ago. He took a leave of absence to care for her and when he came back he was a changed man. Bitter, snapping at everyone. At first we just accepted it as part of the grieving process and thought he'd calm down with time. But it only got worse. He became intolerable. Students avoided him and no one wanted to organize excavations with him. Even his long-term collaborators ditched him."

There was a pause. Remi shook her head. All academic departments were the same. Everyone loved to gossip. She wondered what kind of things had been said behind her back. Actually, she didn't need to wonder. She could imagine clearly enough.

"So he resigned?" Remi asked.

"No, he was fired. The dean brought him into his office one day and suggested he take another leave of absence and get some counseling, and you know what that idiot did? Assaulted the dean! Gave him a concussion and ten stitches! The dean was only trying to help."

"Is he in prison?"

"No. The dean didn't press charges, but of course they fired him. I have no idea where he is now. Find someone else for your research question. Professor Ogden is unhinged. I … all right, I'm being a bit unfair. The man went through a lot. I lost my mother to a long bout of cancer so I know what it's like. But assault? That's unacceptable."

"Do you know anyone who might know where he is?"

"I'm not sure. After he got fired, he cut himself off from the academic community. Really, don't call him. I think he's seriously unbalanced."

"Thank you," Remi said.

"Sorry to have to give you so much bad news. Good luck with your research."

The UCLA professor hung up.

Remi turned to Daniel. "That expensive phone call Resource Management is going to complain about might just have solved the case. The original archaeologist who found the mechanism had a wife who died of cancer and then he assaulted his own dean."

"With a hammer?" Daniel asked.

"His colleague didn't say, but she did say the dean suffered a concussion."

"Good enough. Give me any details you have on the guy and I'll put it through the system. It's night time in the States but hopefully we can still get a court order to search his travel records."

"How long will that take?"

"Too long, I'm afraid," Daniel said, getting on his phone.

CHAPTER TWENTY FIVE

When Daniel's cell phone rang it tore him out of a heavy sleep. He turned over, found himself in a bed instead of the back of an unmarked police car, and for a groggy moment wondered what happened.

Then he remembered. At the crack of dawn, their Swedish colleagues had driven them to a hotel for some much-needed rest. He fumbled for his phone and mumbled a hello.

"Special Agent Walker? This is Special Agent Updike. We cleared your request for a phone trace and travel records on a Professor Tyler Ogden."

Daniel sat up. "Yeah?"

"We're sending you that info now. As you suspected, he flew to Europe a week ago. First England, then Spain, then Copenhagen."

"Bingo."

Daniel fumbled around with his free hand, found the light, and switched it on. A clock told him it was seven-thirty in the morning. He'd gotten two hours of sleep. Typical.

The FBI agent stateside went on. "We've sent his phone information to the Swedish and Danish police. They should be tracking him now."

"Thanks a million, bud. This is going to break the case." Daniel hung up and immediately called the central number for the Uppsala police station the officers had given them the night before.

He was put on hold for a minute, giving him a chance to get dressed. At last an officer who knew the case got on the line.

"We've traced his phone. He's on the morning train to Kiruna."

"Where's that?"

"The far north. He won't arrive for another three hours."

"Does the train stop?"

"He took the express."

"Of course he did," Daniel grumbled.

"We're calling the railway and having them make a stop. Police will be waiting at the station."

"Good. Do you have a photo?"

"The FBI sent one."

"Perfect. Remember that you should treat him as extremely dangerous."

"We will."

The Swede hung up.

Daniel sat back down on the bed, feeling relieved and yet vaguely unsatisfied. The best part of an investigation was when you made the collar, when you finally threw the scumbag down on the ground and slapped the cuffs on him. He had been jealous of Officer De Geer doing that with Sverdrup, at least until the poor guy proved he wasn't the killer. Now he felt jealous of the team that would storm the train.

No way he could get up there in time to play a part. The train must be miles away, speeding for the far north.

What a pity.

Daniel yawned and rubbed his eyes. Should he go back to sleep? Impossible. The prospect of grabbing the killer had gotten him too worked up. He'd go down to the cafeteria, get a strong coffee and a heap of whatever Swedish people ate for breakfast. He hoped they had good Danishes. Sure, that was Denmark, but Swedes must have Danishes too, right?

And he'd let Remi sleep. She'd earned it. When she woke up he could surprise her with a prisoner. She'd feel let down about not making the collar too, but he'd make it up to her with dinner somewhere. He'd ask the concierge for a recommendation for one of those snooty restaurants she liked.

There you go flirting again. You got to stop that.

He took out his phone and texted Veronica.

"Looks like this case is going to wrap up soon. Hopefully I'll be back in a couple of days."

His finger paused over "send," then he added "miss you" and hit it.

As he dressed, a question nagged at him, a question he couldn't find the willpower to answer. Not even to himself.

Do I miss her?

* * *

The call came as he finished his third coffee and second Danish. Uppsala police central station.

"Special Agent Walker here," he said, hearing the eagerness in his voice.

"Bad news, Agent Walker. Our colleagues stormed the train but didn't find him. He bought a ticket with his credit card but he must have left the train before it departed. The only thing we found was his phone hidden in the bathroom."

"Damn it!"

Several of the other guests looked over at him. Daniel ignored them.

"Sorry, sir. We're instituting a broad search throughout town."

"Send his information to every police department in the country."

"We've already done that, sir. And we're continuing to monitor his credit card."

"He won't use that again, now that he's onto us. Keep me informed."

"Yes, sir."

Daniel hung up. Cursing to himself, he slugged back the last of his coffee, snatched a final Danish from the buffet, and hurried upstairs to wake Remi.

He was still wiping crumbs off his mouth when Remi opened up.

She was in her pajamas with the puffy, half-closed eyes of interrupted (and insufficient) sleep. Even so, she looked pretty cute.

Stay focused, dumbass.

He took a deep breath and said. "We lost Tyler Ogden."

Remi snapped to full wakefulness. "What? How?"

"He knows we're onto him. He ditched his phone on a train. The guy must have been watching the house, waiting for the stargazers to leave so he could kill Sverdrup like he killed the others. Then he must have spotted us going in to arrest him, or spotted the cop car that came later to search and guard the house. Just like you thought."

"Damn it!"

"That's what I said. He's not going to use his credit card at this point, but sooner or later we'll nab him. He'll have to cross a border, use his passport."

"He doesn't have to show his passport within the European Union. He can go anywhere from Portugal to Greece."

For a moment they stared at each other. Like so many times before, Daniel could see that spark in her eyes that showed she was thinking the same thing he was.

"Do you think he'd go to Greece?" he asked.

Remi thought for another moment. "It's familiar territory for him. He's been digging there for years, so he probably speaks the language. Modern Greek isn't much of a jump from Ancient Greek, and we know he's fluent in that. Yes, he'd be better able to hide there than anywhere else."

"And the coast is rife with smugglers," Daniel added. "He could get a boat to Turkey or Lebanon, slip away from us entirely."

Remi snapped her fingers. "Wait!"

She ran to the desk where she kept her laptop and files and started rummaging through the original report they had been given at the start of the case.

"Foreign archaeologists digging in Greece—well, most places actually—usually link up with a local archaeologist. Yes, the field report lists as assistant director a Athanasios Vasilakis, Professor at the University of Peloponnese in Corinth."

Daniel felt his stomach twist. He'd been to Corinth. "Uncle" Roy had taken him on a tour of the ancient city while his mother did some research at the university library. Her mom's boyfriend had taken him to the old city ruins, the temple, and then taken him all the way up a steep hill to the Crusader castle of Acrocorinth.

Then he had taken him in one of the towers. Daniel had been thirteen.

Sick bastard.

"You all right?" Remi asked.

Daniel shook himself. "Yeah. Just tired. OK, so he might go to Greece, but why contact his old dig buddy? That UCLA professor you talked to said he burned all his bridges."

Remi paced. "Vasilakis is the only other Ph.D. archaeologist who got to see the device before it was stolen from the excavation shed. They must have discussed its potential, especially after it disappeared. If Ogden confided his thoughts on the healing properties of the device to anyone, it would have been to Vasilakis."

"And Ogden knows we have the final piece. Without that, he can't reconstruct the device. He might make Vasilakis help him."

“He might. Ogden has the original photos, he has all the research he’s done, and he has three out of the four pieces. Sverdrup’s section was only three gears. With a bit of work, Ogden could recreate the device.”

Daniel nodded, his enthusiasm banishing bitter childhood memories. “But he doesn’t have time because he knows we’re hunting him. We’re bound to track him down sooner or later. So he’ll want to rush the job by bringing in the only other person who knows as much about the original device as he does.”

“The only other person he hasn’t killed, at any rate,” Remi said, her voice grim.

“Yeah, and if this Vasilakis guy doesn’t cooperate, he’ll get killed with a hammer just like the rest of them.”

They got to work.

CHAPTER TWENTY SIX

Remi looked up the number for the University of Peloponnese and called while Daniel got in contact with the Greek police. In the back of her mind she realized that she should feel embarrassed standing there in her pajamas, but found that she did not. Daniel was a familiar presence, a comforting one. They worked so well together, and had saved each other's lives on more than one occasion, so what was the harm in him seeing her in her pajamas?

Except the way he looked at her out of the corner of his eye was anything but professional …

Unprofessional, yes, but not creepy. She had endured many hungry stares throughout university, graduate school, and at conferences. As she grew older and her company more refined, those stares became less obvious, better hidden, and yet all the more creepy for it.

Daniel's looks were different. As he talked to some Greek police official on the phone, having to speak slowly and repeat himself to overcome the officer's bad English, he would keep glancing at her out of the corner of his eye. He would only do so for a moment before looking away. Remi got the impression that he didn't look away because he feared getting caught; he looked away because he realized he shouldn't be looking. That spoke well of him.

I really should be embarrassed by this.

The operator at the University of Peloponnese patching her through to the office of Professor Vasilakis disrupted that line of thought. A deep male voice answered in Greek.

"Hello, I'm Special Agent Remi Laurent with the FBI. Is this Professor Athanasios Vasilakis?"

"It is," the man said, switching to English.

"Has Professor Tyler Ogden been in touch with you?"

"No. Why? What's he done now?"

The same reaction as that professor at UCLA.

"He's suspected of a series of murders related to the clockwork mechanism you excavated several years ago."

Vasilakis groaned, as if he had suspected something like this would happen.

"My God, that madman has certainly done it this time. What a mess he made of a good life."

"When was the last time you had contact with Professor Ogden?"

"More than a year ago. Do you know about the circumstances surrounding his losing his job?"

"Yes."

"Well, at first he looked for more work, but of course no American university would hire him. Then he asked if he could guest lecture here. I had heard about how he had assaulted a colleague so I put him off. I pretended to try and get him a post and then said the department lacked the funding to hire him."

"So he didn't find work anywhere?"

"Not to my knowledge. He spent all his time doing more research into the mechanism. It became a quest for him. He asked me to forward him several papers from older Greek journals that weren't accessible online, articles about similar devices and the ancient Greek musicology."

Daniel shouting into the phone distracted her. She put a finger in her ear and asked,

"Did he share with you what he thought of the device?"

"Yes. He said that his research had shown that the device really might work. Ridiculous, of course, and yet he was determined to prove it to the world. He flew into a rage when I told him he was being foolish. He had gotten all the help from me he needed and so he cut me off."

"He might want more help, Professor Vasilakis."

"How so?"

"He's managed to track down three of the four stolen pieces, killing the collectors who had purchased them on the black market. We stopped him from getting the fourth. Now that he can't complete the device, he might come to you to help him finish the job. You're the only other trained archaeologist who saw all the pieces, aren't you?"

"Except for a couple of graduate students, yes. I'm certainly the most qualified. We only had the device in the shed for a couple of days before we had that break-in. They took everything of value. Pottery, several fibulae, a sword … terrible. I hate antiquities thieves. The pieces of the device were the only truly irreparable loss. Such an important item! Revolutionary to our understanding of ancient Greek science."

"They're all recovered now, Professor Vasilakis. All safe in evidence lockers in various police departments. After all this is done, you'll have the chance to study it again."

"That will take years, I'm afraid. Many long years of police and government bureaucracy to bring the pieces back home to Greece." Remi could hear the regret in his voice. It must be terrible to make such a find and have it snatched from you before you got a chance to study it.

"Well, I have some good news for you. One of the victims made extensive notes about the device based on years of research. I have it with me."

"Oh, that would be most interesting," he said, sounding happier. "So what do you want me to do?"

"My partner is talking with the police in Corinth. They'll protect you. Wait one moment." Daniel shaking his head and waving his hand at her made her pull the phone away. "What is it?"

"The local cops aren't going to help," Daniel said.

"What? Why not?"

"They say the evidence is too thin. They're busy with drug smugglers and human traffickers. I worried this would happen. Greece has a long coastline and it's a gateway to Europe. Corinth is a port. The police say they have their hands full trying to stop all the small boats carrying drugs and migrants. Then there's the regular crime. They say they don't have the manpower to protect a university professor who might be threatened by some crazy American. That was the term they used. Crazy American."

"The fools! Can't they see the threat Ogden poses?"

"I tried to explain to them. They didn't listen."

Remi got back on the phone with Athanasios Vasilakis. "I'm terribly sorry, but it looks like your local police department doesn't share our concern."

"They're not going to protect me?"

"It appears not. Is there anywhere you can go?"

Vasilakis thought for a moment. "My parents' house. It's in a village not far from here. Ogden doesn't know about it. I'll cancel my classes and go there. But how long to I have to hide?"

"We're coming down to Greece," she said, hoping Resource Allocation agreed with that idea. "We will do everything in our power to apprehend him. I promise. Please give me your mobile number so we can keep in touch."

He gave it and Remi called it so he'd have her number. She also forwarded Daniel's number.

"Please keep me updated," the Greek archaeologist said. "I'll leave within the hour. I'll call if I hear from Ogden."

"Thank you, professor Vasilakis." Remi hung up.

She turned to Daniel, infuriated.

"How can the Corinth police be so stupid?"

Daniel raised a calming hand. "They're not being stupid. They're prioritizing. They have a lot on their plate and given the Greek financial crisis they're probably underfunded and understaffed. They're concentrating on stopping the crimes they know are being committed, instead of the crimes they think might be committed."

"But Ogden has killed three people!"

"And there's no solid evidence he'll try to kill Vasilakis, or even come to Greece. We're working on a hunch. Your hunches generally turn out right, but the cops down in Greece don't know that."

"That's stupid!"

"No. It makes sense from their point of view. Welcome to policework."

"Ugh!" Remi threw her hands in the air.

Daniel smiled. "I'm going back to my room and deal with Resource Allocation. They're probably going to be tougher to convince than the Greek cops. In the meantime, why don't you get dressed and get some breakfast. They have strong coffee, and six different types of Danish. Or are they Swedes?"

"How can you joke at a time like this?" Remi grumbled. The whole case might come unraveled thanks to lack of care on the part of the authorities.

"It keeps me sane."

Daniel's phone buzzed.

"A message from the Uppsala police. Damn, more bad news. A car was stolen this morning just a block away from the train station and out of sight of the station's security cameras. It disappeared shortly after the train to the north left the station. No witnesses, so no proof, but they're thinking Ogden stole it. Looks like he's going to drive to Greece."

"It's so far. That will take more than a day. Maybe even two days."

"Which means we might get the jump on him, assuming he doesn't ditch the car and grab a high-speed train somewhere. While you're eating breakfast, check out what high-speed lines go to Athens. We'll get the local police to keep a lookout."

"I will."

"Wish me luck with Resource Allocation. I'm going to need it."

Daniel left the room. Remi hurried to dress and get back to work.

CHAPTER TWENTY SEVEN

Another flight, another country. Another rented car.

Daniel had called ahead for this one, using FBI money before he returned the damaged Swedish car in a so far successful bid to keep Resource Allocation from cutting off their funds. They must have seen the damage bill by now, though, because they had sent three texts that Daniel had ignored.

She felt sorry for him, and relieved for herself. As the senior agent, he would take the blame. Being rated only a trainee agent turned out to have some unexpected privileges.

They had left the western suburbs of Athens and its snarling traffic far behind. Now they drove through stunning countryside. Rough, rocky hills rose above verdant valleys, and everywhere they could see signs of the past. A medieval castle atop a steep eminence. An ancient temple overlooking a rushing stream. An aqueduct from the time when Rome ruled over its older cousin. An olive grove stretched to their right, and Remi spied an old man herding a flock of fluffy white sheep between the trees.

They passed through villages of whitewashed houses with red tiled roofs shining in the sunlight, and every now and then the landscape would open up to their left and they'd see the glittering expanse of the Mediterranean.

She loved Greece. Its stunning beauty and deep history made it one of the most special places in Europe.

Daniel didn't share her enthusiasm. He gripped the wheel, ignoring the beauty all around while muttering indistinctly to himself.

Poor man. He's worried about the bill for the crash. He might get demoted for that. FBI bureaucracy can be as petty as academic bureaucracy.

Remi wondered if he was stressed about Veronica too. She had noticed he had gotten a couple of texts from her. Remi had gotten into the habit of peeking at his phone when he was checking it. How rude and intrusive. She should stop. She had never liked nosey people.

Still, she couldn't quite resist.

They saw a sign for Corinth, and in the distance Remi spied the great castle of Acrocorinth atop a massive stone outcropping overlooking the gulf and city below. She had visited it many years before. The old acropolis had a history stretching back to prehistoric times. Its most visible ruins were the massive walls built in medieval times and attacked by a succession of invaders—the Byzantines, the Crusaders, the Franks, the Ottomans. The walls were well preserved and you could enter some of the towers and climb up for some splendid views.

When they had finally captured Ogden, Remi hoped they'd have time to go up there. Daniel would probably like it. Men always liked knights and castles, whether they were academics or officers of the law. They were all boys at heart.

Remi got out her phone and called Athanasios Vasilakis.

The Greek archaeologist picked up almost immediately.

"Hello. Did you catch him?"

"I'm afraid not, Professor Vasilakis. The Swedish police have reported to us that the car he is suspected of stealing was discovered in Berlin. The car was torched, but the Berlin police were able to read the serial numbers and match it with the car from Sweden. We suspect he got on a train. There's a high-speed line to Athens so he might be coming to Greece."

"Coming? He may be here by now!"

"Did you go to your parents' country cottage?"

"Yes."

"Good. Stay there. We're just coming into Corinth now. We'll consult with the local police. After that, perhaps we can come out to your place."

"I'd rather come in, if you don't mind. My parents are quite frail. They shouldn't get excited or worried. They think I'm simply up for a visit."

"All right. When can you come down?"

"I'm not sure. I'm up here alone since I dismissed the caretaker. She's just a young girl from the village and I didn't want her in danger."

"You're in no danger, Professor Vasilakis, as long as no one knows where your parents live."

"A few of my close friends know the village but not the address."

"What about other family members? Anyone in Corinth?"

"I'm divorced. My wife and two sons live in Athens. Ogden doesn't know their address and I've warned them to be careful."

"That's good. We'll be in touch."

When she hung up and turned to consult Daniel, her words froze in her throat. Daniel had been staring up at Acrocorinth, and quickly turned his face away when she got off the phone.

He wasn't quick enough to keep her from seeing the tears in his eyes.

What's going on?

* * *

Many hours later, Remi had grown impatient with everything—impatient with the local police, impatient with Professor Vasilakis, and impatient with her partner.

The local police had been welcoming, bringing them in for coffee and sandwiches and listening with interest to their story of the hunt for Tyler Ogden. Remi got the impression that a visit by a pair of FBI agents was a novelty for them. A female FBI agent was even more of a novelty. She didn't see a female officer during her entire visit to the station.

While the police were sympathetic and had put out an all-points bulletin about Ogden, they said they could do nothing more without a solid lead.

"We have intelligence that several migrant boats will try to come ashore near here tonight," one officer told them. "We must stop them, and that will take up all our manpower except for the most minimum number to patrol the city."

Remi had also grown impatient with the Greek academic they had come here to protect. He had not answered two different calls, replying only with texts that he was busy caring for his parents. A demand from Daniel to prove that he was alive and well and not under duress finally earned them a video call.

Athanasios Vasilakis was a portly man with a large curly black beard threaded with gray. His hair was receding and his face had the deep tan and crow's feet of a man accustomed to working outside.

"Yes, I am alive and not under duress, my friends," he said, sounding a bit annoyed. He moved his phone camera around so they could see the modest interior of a country cottage. A frail-looking couple sat together on a sofa in the far background, the man with a cane and black cap that seemed to be the regulation uniform of old men in Greece, the woman wearing a print dress and busy knitting. Vasilakis stood well away from them and kept his voice down. The woman called out something in Greek and Vasilakis shouted a response.

"As you can see, I have my hands full here. Sorry, but they require much care. I need to go now and prepare them a meal. I'm afraid I can't get down to Corinth like I said."

"Can we come up?" Remi asked.

"Later tonight. Then we can talk." He hung up.

Remi grumbled. They didn't even know what village he was in.

Daniel was also being a bother. He had been in a bad mood ever since they had gotten to Greece, vacillating between being withdrawn and irritable. Remi had no idea what was going on. Veronica? The FBI harassing him? Whatever it was, he had cut off every attempt Remi had made to draw him out. Eventually she gave up. If he didn't want to talk about it, she didn't see what she could do, and yet she worried he was too distracted from the case.

At last, as the sun set and sleep began to tug her under, they got a call from Vasilakis.

"My parents will be going to sleep soon. They always go to bed early but get up several times in the night, as old people do. It would be best if you come up right away. It's about half an hour outside of the city. I look forward to discussing the device with you."

Finally! Remi thought. *It's nice that he cares so much for his parents, but this delay has grown from understandable to ridiculous.*

"Send me a location on Google Maps and we'll be right up," Remi replied.

"I'm sending it now, and please bring up that notebook you mentioned. I'd be most interested in looking at it. Perhaps I can give you some insight into what Ogden might do next."

"That would be perfect, thank you."

They headed out. Corinth is a small city of fewer than 50,000 people and it did not take long before they were in the darkness of the countryside. Remi found herself dropping off to sleep. While she had gotten a few hours of sleep the night before in Sweden and napped a bit on the plane, she was still far, far behind on rest. It seemed their cases always ran them ragged.

Daniel certainly felt the strain. He had remained in a bad mood all day.

Remi let him drive and rested her head against the seat. Her thoughts grew fuzzy and she fell into a dream. It came as brief flashes of images. The catacombs. Remi opening an old chest but unable to see what was inside. A crying old man. Daniel cursing and kicking at the walls of Acrocorinth until they came tumbling down. The cryptex, locked again. When Remi tried to unlock it, the combination no longer worked. In her sleep, she felt a rising panic.

Daniel's voice came to her. "We're here."

Where? Her sleeping mind wondered.

"We're here," Daniel said again.

Remi rubbed her eyes and opened them. She found they had parked in front of a stone cottage, its whitewashed wall glowing in the headlights. Looking around, she saw a few other cottages scattered across the hilly surroundings, none of them close. A small patch of light in the valley below must have been the village Vasilakis had spoken about. It looked at least two kilometers away.

"Our friend's parents sure live in the middle of nowhere," Daniel said. "It's a good place for him to hide out."

"Yes, at least he's safe," Remi yawned. "I hope he has some insight into where his colleague disappeared to."

"We'll soon find out."

The front door had opened and a heavyset but muscular looking man stood there, wearing jeans and a dress shirt. It took Remi a moment to recognize him as Athanasios Vasilakis. People always looked different in real life than on a video call.

Daniel switched off the car and they got out. Remi noticed a Jeep parked nearby, but no other vehicle. His parents must have been past the age of driving. She wondered what they did all day up here.

"Welcome," Vasilakis said, shaking their hands. "Why don't you come in and I'll serve you a drink. Did you bring the notebook?"

"Yes, we did," Remi said, holding it out for him.

He smiled. "Excellent. It's just what we needed."

“Yes, it’s just what we needed,” said a male voice behind them. He spoke with an American accent.

They turned, and saw Tyler Ogden gripping a double-barreled shotgun, aimed right at them.

CHAPTER TWENTY EIGHT

Remi froze. Daniel moved his hand for the inside of his jacket and Ogden clicked his tongue.

"None of that," he said. Daniel's hand stopped in mid-motion. "Athanasios, check them for weapons."

Now that she got a better look at the gun, she saw it was old and battered, probably the property of the couple whose cottage this was. Still, it seemed frightening enough pointed at her.

Vasilakis stepped up behind Daniel and reached into his jacket. Just as he did, Daniel dropped to the ground, spun, and landed a punch right in the Greek professor's crotch.

An unsporting move, but given the betrayal, a justifiable one. Vasilakis let out an anguished grunt and doubled over. Daniel rolled into him, undercutting his legs and making him the Greek man on top of him. Remi realized that was to shield himself from Ogden's shotgun.

Remi reached into her vest where her shoulder holster was hidden. She got it halfway out before the twin barrels of the shotgun loomed up before her face like a pair of malignant eyes.

"Drop it," Ogden ordered.

She tensed, then dropped the gun.

Daniel and Vasilakis still struggled on the ground, Daniel pummeling him with one hand while trying to draw his gun with the other.

"Stop that or your partner gets it," Ogden snapped.

Daniel looked over Vasilakis's bulky form and saw Remi with the shotgun to her face. He snarled.

"Killing a fed will get you the chair, Ogden."

"Not if they don't know," he said. "There's plenty of hunting in this region. A gunshot will be ignored. Now hand over your gun. Two fingers only, please, and keep your other hand clear."

Vasilakis got off of Daniel, grabbed one of his wrists, and waited as Daniel slowly pulled his gun out of his shoulder holster, using only two fingers so it would be impossible to maneuver it to fire. Vasilakis snatched it from him with his free hand, then backed away, still moving stiffly from the punch to his groin.

"You'll never get away with this," Remi said. "The Corinthian police know we're here and they know who you are. It won't take them long to figure out what happened if we disappear."

"We don't need much time," Ogden said, gesturing with his shotgun for Daniel to rise. Vasilakis kept Daniel's gun leveled at him as he did so.

"Why are you doing this?" Remi asked the Greek professor.

A dry, croaking voice from inside the house interrupted him before he could reply. Vasilakis called out in Greek, moving to the door. He put Daniel's gun behind his back. With a warning glance, Ogden moved the shotgun down so it looked like he was casually standing with it.

The old man Remi had seen in the video call came to the doorway, wearing pajamas and slippers and looked at them curiously with watery eyes. He asked a question in Greek. Vasilakis said something reassuring and walked him back inside.

As soon as they disappeared, Ogden took a step back and leveled his shotgun once again.

Vasilakis came back out. "You asked why we're doing this. You just saw the answer. My father is suffering from a bad heart. The doctors say he could die at any time. He used to be such a strong man. I'd see him out ploughing the fields or tending the orchards. He was the best farmer in the district. Ask anyone old enough to remember. But now? Just look at him. Half blind. Half deaf. At the grave's edge. My mother too is as frail as a bird. She suffers from a number of complaints. And as for myself … well, I have diabetes. I've read enough about it to know the slow decline many people with diabetes endure."

"That will all be cured once we build the device," Ogden told him.

"God, I hope so." Vasilakis walked over to where Ramon-Diaz's journal had fallen on the ground, picked it up, and brushed it off as if it was a holy book.

He held it up to the light coming from the open door and started to flip through it, eyes going wide.

"Yes, Tyler. Look, it's all here!" Vasilakis looked at Remi and Daniel, who Ogden had herded together against the wall as if for a firing squad. "You see, the Spaniard knew some things we didn't. In the early part of the twentieth century an excavation at Empúries, an ancient Greek colony on the Spanish coast, uncovered parts of a similar device that gave clues to how to reconstruct this one. But the excavation was published in an report in the 1920s. It got forgotten. It was never put online and even if it had been, neither of us read Spanish. Now we don't need to. He drew it all right here."

The Greek professor's father called from the house again. Vasilakis replied, saying something impatient. Then he turned to Ogden.

"Let's get them out of here before he comes out again."

Ogden jerked the shotgun toward the side of the cottage. "Go around the house. There's a workshop out back. And don't try anything or I'll shoot both of you down like dogs."

You're going to do that anyway, Remi thought.

Her heart hammered in her chest. She felt a cold, rising panic that she struggled to contain. All her instincts told her to run, or throw herself at these men's feet and beg for her life.

The rational part of her mind knew neither of those actions would save her.

Forcing herself to act calm even though on the inside she felt like falling apart, Remi turned to looked Vasilakis in the eye. "What would your parents think of you doing this?"

Vasilakis hesitated a second, his gaze slipping away, and then he stood a little straighter. "They're farmers. Practical people. They'd hate me killing you, but love the fact that I'd be saving millions."

"You're not a murderer," Remi said, "and you're not a madman."

"Quiet," Ogden growled, jabbing the shotgun into Remi's back and making her cry out. "Move around the cottage."

They walked. Daniel kept a slow pace, his eyes darting around. Remi know he was trying to find an escape, a way to strike back. She didn't see anything. Ogden walked just out of reach behind them, and Vasilakis walked a little behind Ogden, gripping Daniel's gun and carrying Remi's in his belt.

"Where are we going?" Remi asked.

"My father's old workshop," Vasilakis said. "He used to be handy with machine tools. Fixed all his own farm equipment and those of the neighbors. Such a proud man. So strong. I've been working there myself, and now that Tyler has arrived he will be helping me reconstruct the last of the gears."

Suddenly, Remi saw her fate. They would be put up against a wall in the workshop, some power tool would be turned on to mask the noise, and they'd be shot. Mr. and Mrs. Vasilakis, both nearly deaf, wouldn't hear the shots over the noise of the tools, or if they did they wouldn't dream their dutiful son, a respectable university professor, had just committed cold-blooded murder.

"I'm sorry," Daniel whispered.

He knows too.

Remi reached out a hand and their fingers interlaced.

"What are you trying to do?" Ogden snapped. "Stay apart!"

Remi let his hand go, feeling an ache in her heart with the terrible knowledge that she wouldn't touch him or anyone else ever again.

They came to the back corner of the cottage.

"Go left," Ogden ordered.

Remi saw their chance. Just as they went around the corner, the workshop coming into view, Ogden stepped a bit away from the edge of the cottage to remain in sight, but Vasilakis temporarily disappeared from view.

Remi spun, ready to fling herself at Ogden. He'd shoot her, but Daniel might survive.

She didn't get a chance. Daniel shoved her aside and leapt on Ogden. Remi shouted as the American archaeologist pulled the trigger, sure that her partner and friend would be blown apart the next instant.

Nothing happened except an ineffectual click. The farmer's old shotgun had misfired.

Daniel didn't let him have the chance to try again. He slammed into Ogden and gave him a vicious right hook. Remi rushed forward, knowing she would have only a second before Vasilakis came around that corner.

Ogden went down, Daniel above him and pummeling him in the face with one hand while holding the barrel of the shotgun with the other. Ogden pulled on the gun, trying to wrench it free, and smacked Daniel in the mouth with the barrel, his lips bursting open and gouting blood. Remi saw a rock by the cottage and grabbed it. By the time she stood up, Vasilakis had appeared around the corner.

Vasilakis stared at her a moment, the pistol in his hand pointed right at her chest.

Although the light was dim, only what shone through the curtains of a back window, she could see the hesitation in his eyes. He stared at the two men struggling, Daniel with blood pouring down the front of his shirt, still slamming away at Ogden who hadn't managed to get off the ground, and Remi holding a rock the side of a baseball in her hand.

"Stop!" he shouted. Daniel ignored him. Remi, staring at the muzzle of the pistol, didn't dare move.

"I said stop!" Vasilakis pointed the gun in the air and fired.

Remi didn't see if Daniel stopped or not, because the instant the gun pointed away from her, she leapt forward and smacked Vasilakis on the side of the head. He fell with a groan, the gun falling from his hand. Remi scooped it up, yanked the second pistol from the Greek man's belt, and turned to the two men still struggling.

She stepped over to them and pointed both pistols in Ogden's face.

"Stop."

Ogden's eyes, half closed from the pummeling he'd received, studied her for a moment. Remi moved the pistols a little closer to him.

"Stop or you're dead."

Ogden slumped, letting go of the shotgun. Daniel pulled it away, then pounded the butt into the American's stomach. Ogden curled up, coughing.

"Get Vasilakis," Daniel said, pulling out a set of handcuffs from his ruined suit flipping Ogden over, and cuffing him.

Remi turned and found Vasilakis had managed to get to his knees, one hand cradling a bleeding bump on his head. He looked up at her.

"I told you that you weren't a killer," Remi said. "You could have shot me and then Daniel, and you hesitated."

Vasilakis didn't reply.

"You're still going to jail," Remi went on. "Get on the ground and put your hands behind your back."

A gasp made them all turn.

Vasilakis's father stood there, face white, mouth hanging open. He croaked out a question. Vasilakis said something and the old man staggered back, hand clutching his heart.

He let out another gasp, sounding choked, and fell hard on the ground.

“No!” Vasilakis shouted, rushing for him.

Daniel was there in an instant, trying to perform CPR. Vasilakis didn’t run or fight, he merely knelt by his father, moaning “No! No!”

His mother came out a moment later. For a moment, Remi worried she might collapse as well, but thankfully she was made of stronger stuff and didn’t do anything more than stand there, asking questions that went unanswered as tears streamed down her wrinkled cheeks.

Daniel tried to revive him for several minutes, but old man Vasilakis was beyond saving, killed by the shock of seeing what his son had turned into.

CHAPTER TWENTY NINE

Washington, D.C., three days later ...

Daniel, a bottle of Spanish red wine tucked under his arm, took a deep breath and rang what used to be his doorbell. Now it Veronica's doorbell. She had gotten the house in a suburb of D.C. as part of the divorce settlement. He could have used his keys—he had kept a spare set that for nostalgic reasons that he had never told Veronica about—but he decided that wouldn't get the evening off to a good start.

Veronica answered within a couple of seconds, showing she had been waiting near the door. Daniel blinked. She looked great. She wore a red satin dress (satin had always driven him crazy) and an emerald necklace he had given her for their fifth anniversary.

She smiled. It was the first real smile she had given him in a long time.

"You brought the Spanish wine," she said.

He gave a mock bow. "As you commanded, madam."

Daniel neglected to tell her he had bought it in a duty free shop in Stockholm while he and Remi had waited for their flight to Athens. Since Sweden didn't produce wine, the shop had carried wine from countries that did.

A shadow passed over Veronica's face.

"You've been hurt again." She made it sound like an accusation.

Daniel's hand went up to his lip. "Oh this? A murderer hit me with the barrel of an old shotgun. At least he didn't slug me over the head with a hammer. That was his M.O."

"Could we not talk about your grisly work?"

You asked.

Veronica drew close and gave him a lingering kiss. He responded willingly, despite his lip singing with pain. At least the rest of his body felt good. Daniel's hand reached to touch her side.

Should I move it up? Or down? Better just leave it in place.

"Did that hurt?" she asked once she finally pulled away.

"No. In fact, it feels better."

An old joke. He'd come back from cases beaten up on several occasions, and Veronica would always "kiss it to make it better." Then she'd bitch at him for having such a dangerous job. "You could do anything with your life," she'd say. "Why do this?"

Because of what happened in Corinth, he'd like to say, *the first and second time.*

That was what he'd like to say, but he'd never gotten up the nerve to tell her about his first visit there, and he sure wasn't going to ruin the evening by telling her about the second.

But she didn't follow up with the usual complaint. No, she was in a reconciliatory mood tonight.

She had even cooked, judging from the roast chicken smell wafting out of what used to be his kitchen. Cooking wasn't Veronica's strong suit, not that he was one to judge. Being partnered up with a Frenchwoman acted as a constant reminder that he had no taste in cuisine.

I just have simple taste. Nothing wrong with that.

They went into the dining room where Veronica had laid out a white tablecloth and two tall candles. A photo of them at the Grand Canyon a couple of years back sat on the side table. He noticed it had shifted from its old location a few inches to the right, and that a couple of decorative porcelain figurines she liked to collect (*talk about bad taste!*) were bunched to the side.

The figurines were new acquisitions, and had obviously been sitting where the photo, newly replaced in its more-or-less original position, now stood. That meant the figurines had been shoved to one end of the side table. That wasn't orderly. Veronica loved everything orderly.

So you put away the photo and only put it back because I was coming over. Never try to hide anything from a cop, honey.

Daniel suppressed his annoyance. She was making an effort, and so should he.

That kiss sure had been nice. Maybe there'd be more.

He picked up the bottle opener sitting on the table, opened the wine, and poured it into two glasses they had gotten as a wedding gift. Austrian crystal. Remi would have approved. Well, maybe not. Austrian were practically Germans and the French didn't like Germans.

It reminded him of the old joke—"Why are the streets of Paris lined with trees? Because the Germans like to march in the shade."

He had never told her that joke. She probably wouldn't laugh. Europeans. No sense of humor.

Daniel poured the wine and they both picked up a glass. Veronica held hers high.

"So what shall we toast?" she asked.

"Um, I don't know."

"How about new beginnings?" Veronica suggested.

"Sure." The trace of a frown creased her brow. He put some enthusiasm in his voice. "Yeah, that's great! To new beginnings."

They touched glasses, the fine crystal making a musical tone.

I wonder what illness that sound cures? Crazy Greeks.

They each took a sip. Veronica made appreciative noises. Daniel nodded in agreement.

"Beats the cheap stuff," he said.

Veronica sat. "The chicken will be done in twenty minutes. Let's talk a bit."

Daniel sat too.

"This is really nice," Daniel said, not sure how to start a conversation that he knew would be awkward.

"We should have done this more," Veronica agreed.

"We can. From now on."

Veronica gave him an uncertain smile. "The way the Antiquities Division has you globetrotting, we'll sample all the world's wine."

"We'll have to be careful not to turn into drunks." Daniel took another sip of his wine.

Veronica grew serious. "I've been doing a lot of thinking, and I realize I've been too hard on you for your workload. I mean, you're helping people. Saving people. I won't lie, I still hate how it takes you away so much and how it puts you in danger. Just look at your lip! But I've been unfair. What you do is important. All I do is make money for the boss."

"You've worked hard."

"Until they stopped promoting me. I'm not going anywhere in that company. I still put in the time but you know how I've been getting out more. I wish you could join me."

"I'm free tomorrow. Why don't you take me on one of those hikes you're always talking about?"

Veronica smiled, but that smile quickly faded. "All right. But … I need to talk to you about something."

Oh crap. This sounds serious. Did she sleep with someone?

Veronica went on.

"The other big problem is about having children."

Daniel grimaced. He couldn't have kids. Low sperm count. Veronica felt a deep need to have children.

She must have seen his reaction because she hurried to continue. "I've thought of a compromise. You want to adopt but I want to have a child. You can't understand a woman's needs. It's not your fault. Men are different. When woman gets to a certain age, they realize that career and friends aren't enough. I want to start a family. And adoption isn't the same."

Back to the same old argument. Giving a child a good home would make him feel better about the crappy home he grew up in. Working in law enforcement, he knew all about the dangers of the foster care system. If he could save some kid from the instability of being shuffled between foster homes, and the risks of abuse that entailed, it would be like he was balancing the scales.

But he couldn't explain that to Veronica. She knew he had a rift with his mother, but she didn't know why. And he didn't have the courage to tell her why. He'd rather charge at a madman gripping a shotgun than do that.

"I've done some research," Veronica said. "And I could get artificially inseminated. I've found a good clinic that screens donors and—"

"You want me to raise another man's kid?" He couldn't believe his ears.

"Adopting would be raising another man's kid."

"But the kid already exists and needs a home!"

"Yes, but it wouldn't be our child."

"If you get a sperm donor, it wouldn't be our child, it would be yours and his."

"We could raise it as our own. Look, I have some brochures."

She went to the side table and opened a drawer below the photo of them at the Grand Canyon and pulled out several colorful brochures of smiling couples holding newborn babies. She started explaining the process, flipping through the pages and getting more and more enthusiastic.

The words passed over Daniel like so much white noise. The pictures of happy new parents went unseen. There was no way he'd do this. If he was going to become a father, he would save a kid who needed saving, not help his ex-wife bring some stranger's kid into the world. He didn't have a moral objection if that's what other couples wanted to do, but this wasn't for him and never would be.

Looking at her eager, happy face, he knew in his gut that this was what Veronica would do, with or without him.

And at that moment he knew it was well and truly over.

Somehow he would make it through this dinner, and that would be that. There would be no hike tomorrow, and they would not sample the world's wine.

It was over.

CHAPTER THIRTY

Georgetown University, the next day

Remi rubbed her bloodshot eyes and stifled a yawn. It was never good form to yawn in front of the dean, even if he was no longer your dean since you had left the university and joined the FBI.

Ronald Hines, Dean of Arts and Sciences at Georgetown, smiled from across his desk. A window behind him looked out on the quad, where trees exploded with autumnal colors.

"Jetlag?" he asked.

"Is it so obvious?" Remi said with a smile.

Actually she was mostly over her jetlag, except that she had been pulling long hours examining the medallion they had retrieved from the catacombs.

He smiled back. "Yes. You should have told me you just got back from Europe when I asked you in."

"It's fine."

"Still burning the candle at both ends, eh? You'll go as far in the FBI as you have in academia."

Many of Remi's male colleagues would have said that with a touch of sarcasm or jealousy. Not Dean Hines. He was like an American businessman. As long as you produced results, he didn't care what gender you were, what your skin color was, or who you slept with. Publications and good press for the university were all that mattered.

A bit too utilitarian for her taste, but at least she got to skip the condescending remarks and lack of appreciation she received from so many other male academics.

Remi tried and failed to suppress another yawn. Dean Hines took that as a signal to continue. Or "cut to the chase" as he liked to say.

"Let me cut to the chase." *You see?* Remi told herself. "I want you to stay on at Georgetown."

Remi blinked. "What?"

Not the most intelligent response, but she hadn't had a full night's sleep in more than a week.

"The FBI has provided you with a work visa. While that specifically is only to work for them, there's nothing stopping you from giving paid guest lectures on a regular basis. The legal department says we can't actually put you on the list of faculty, but we can have you give any number of invited talks."

Eagerness gave her weary mind a much-needed boost. Surprise followed quick on its heels. She thought she had left academia behind. After long deliberation, and weighing up the safety and success of her old career, and the excitement and promise of a new one, she had chosen crime investigation over historical research.

Now she was being offered the chance to keep her hand in, and it excited her to no end.

"I would love to!" she answered, and then a question arose in her mind, a question she wasn't quite sure how to ask. So she decided to fish. "That's a wonderful idea you had."

Dean Hines smiled. "Trying to retain a successful and increasingly famous scholar is hardly a work of genius. I'm surprised the history department hasn't been battering down my door demanding I do this."

So this wasn't Cyril's idea.

Cyril was the head of the history department, and her former lover. He had broken up with her because of her long absences. At least that's what he told her was the reason. Perhaps he told himself that too.

Remi felt a mingling of hurt and relief that her old lover wasn't trying to get her back. The dean went on.

"We'd like to do, say, one lecture every week if that's possible. We can work around your schedule. Early evenings would be best since more students and faculty would be able to attend. Why don't you think about some possible topics over the next couple of days and then send them to me? Something that mixes your FBI experience with history would be great, and of course the cryptex."

Remi tensed a bit at that.

I'll have to be careful what I say, but of course he would want a lecture on the cryptex. After the Cryptex Killer, there's been so much interest.

"I'd like to keep media presence to a minimum," she said.

The dean nodded. "I thought you'd say that. No reporters. I can't keep them from calling you, though. Has that been a problem?"

"I have a filter on my phone. It only rings for a few numbers."

Like Cyril's. Not that it ever rings for him anymore.

"A wise move. I'm looking forward to hearing your lectures. And thanks for coming in. I'm afraid I can't buy you a coffee. I have a meeting with the Visiting Faculty committee at the History Department."

To pick my replacement, Remi thought with a twinge of regret.

Despite feeling quite sure she had made the right choice with her switch to the FBI, being back on campus brought up a lot of old memories and nostalgia. She had only left her old life a couple of months before, and it still didn't seem entirely real.

She shook hands with the dean and headed out. As she walked down the stairs of the administration building, her phone rang.

For a second her heart did a flip flop thinking it might be Cyril. Had he seen her on campus? What would he want?

She pulled out her phone with a sense of dread. Daniel.

"Hello!" she said, immediately feeling better.

"Hi." In that short, one-syllable greeting she heard sadness and nervousness.

"Are you all right?"

"You at home?"

"I'm just heading there."

"Can I come over for a minute? There's something I want to talk to you about."

She almost asked if they had been given another case, but realized that Daniel's tone spoke of something else entirely. What was wrong? There always seemed to be something wrong with her partner, bubbling just under the surface.

"Of course you can come over. I'll be back there in twenty minutes."

"All right. See you in about half an hour."

He hung up, leaving her utterly bewildered.

* * *

When Daniel came to her door, Remi could see he looked down. More than that, he looked nervous. That startled her. While Daniel could be hot-headed, he always exuded a sense of confidence that she had come to rely on when on their cases.

"Come on in," Remi said. "Would you like some coffee?"

He managed half a smile. "I'm trying to cut down after the gallons we drank on the last case."

"Hmm. That might not be a bad idea. Sit down."

Remi sat on the sofa in her living room. Daniel remained standing. Silence made the air seem heavy.

"How's your lip?" she asked.

Daniel shrugged. "Getting better."

More silence.

What's going on?

Daniel pointed at an envelope lying on her coffee table. Half of it was covered with an ink drawing of Healy Hall, Georgetown's most beautiful building.

"What's that?" he asked.

Remi could tell he was putting off whatever it was he wanted to say. She answered anyway.

"Mail art. I'm sending it to Oskar Sverdrup."

"You drew that? It's good."

"It's all right. I took some drawing classes when I was younger. I haven't tried anything in years."

"It's better than some of the stuff he had."

"I feel bad about what we put him through, and I think he needs a friend."

"You'll end up on his wall. Maybe he'll put you next to that priest's drawing. How is the research going?"

"Excellent. The medallion that priest drew gave me some good clues. The way the lines are inscribed on the medallion and how they relate to rivers, and the style it's all done in, has helped me read the medallion we found. I haven't located the mountain, but it's only a matter of time."

"Have you contacted the priest?"

"I will soon. Want to come to Germany with me? The FBI owes us a two-for-one after calling us back from vacation."

Daniel looked everywhere except at her. "I'm not sure you're going to want me along after I say what I got to say."

"What's wrong?"

"I … I have feelings for you, Remi." The words, so long held back, now came out in a rush. "I know it's unprofessional and I know we totally aren't a match, but there it is. I can't deny it and it's unfair to you not to tell you. They've been growing for a while now. You're amazing. So smart and so brave. And I'm not getting back with Veronica. I had dinner with her last night and we had a long talk and it's just not going to work out. Now you probably think I'm being an idiot talking to you like this—"

"You're not being an idiot."

"—and I know you don't feel the same about me. I'm sorry for holding your hand. That was inappropriate and I—"

"I didn't mind."

That stopped him short. He finally looked at her. Blinked.

"Oh."

Remi wasn't sure what to say next. Silence began to draw out again. Daniel broke it.

"So you're not trying to get back with Cyril?"

"No."

Daniel opened his mouth, seemed to reconsider what he wanted to say and then said, "Look, I'm way out of line here. This is totally unprofessional. If you want to get reassigned to a new partner, talk to the boss. I'm sure it can be arranged. And if you want to stay a team, I'll shut up. You don't want to date a guy like me anyway. Sorry I brought it up, but I'm sure you figured it out. I wanted to clear the air. I'll go now. Sorry to bother you."

He took a step back and started to turn for the door.

"No, wait. It's all right. We should talk about this. I could tell you were having trouble with Veronica. I'm sorry I didn't say anything. You were so upset in Corinth I knew it must have been that."

To her surprise, Daniel went pale. A flicker of emotion passed over his features. What was it? Anger? Anguish? Both?

She didn't get to see what it turned into, because he quickly turned his back on her and hurried to the door.

Remi sat there, stunned. She had never seen him so upset before, and the things he had said …

She felt the same. She hadn't had the courage to put them into words. She hadn't wanted to upset his chance to get back with Veronica.

But now that had ended.

I hope he didn't end it because of me.

No. That marriage had ended well before he even knew me.

Daniel opened the door.

Say something. Say something.

Just as he opened it, mumbling an apology for bothering her, she blurted,

"Why wouldn't I want to date someone like you?"

Of all the things you could have said, you said THAT?

Daniel looked at the floor, shook his head, and went out.

Remi sat where she was, too confused to follow.

NOW AVAILABLE!

THE SEDUCTION CODE

(A Remi Laurent FBI Suspense Thriller—Book 6)

In an ancient abbey in Ireland, once thought to be home to the Knights Templar, a murder has occurred—and a priceless artifact has been stolen. As brilliant history professor teams up with the FBI, she fears the worst: the killer has found the one legitimate lead to the Holy Grail—and will stop at nothing until he finds it.

THE SEDUCTION CODE (A Remi Laurent FBI Suspense Thriller) is book #6 in a new series by mystery and suspense author Ava Strong, which begins with THE DEATH CODE (Book #1).

FBI Special Agent Daniel Walker, 40, known for his ability to hunt killers, his street-smarts, and his disobedience, is singled out from the Behavioral Analysis Unit and assigned to the FBI's new Antiquities unit. The unit, formed to hunt down priceless relics in the global world of antiquities, has no idea how to enter the mind of a murderer.

Remi Laurent, 34, brilliant history professor at Georgetown, is the world's leading expert in obscure historic artifacts. Shocked when the FBI asks for her help to find a killer, she finds herself reluctantly partnered with this rude American FBI agent. Special Agent Walker and Remi Laurent are an unlikely duo, with his ability to enter killers' minds and her unparalleled scholarship, the only thing they have in common, their determination to decode the clues and stop a killer.

Remi and Daniel's search leads them into the ancient abbeys and dark cloisters of the UK countryside in a desperate hunt for the killer. Why is he after the Grail—and why does he seem so confident he can find it?

Who will he kill next?

And will Remi be smart enough to find a relic that has been lost for centuries?

An unputdownable crime thriller featuring an unlikely partnership between a jaded FBI agent and a brilliant historian, the REMI LAURENT series is a riveting mystery, grounded in history, and packed with suspense and revelations that will leave you continuously in shock, and flipping pages late into the night.

Future books in the series will be available soon.

Ava Strong

Bestselling author Ava Strong is author of the REMI LAURENT mystery series, comprising six books (and counting); of the ILSE BECK mystery series, comprising seven books (and counting); of the STELLA FALL psychological suspense thriller series, comprising six books (and counting); and of the DAKOTA STEELE FBI suspense thriller series, comprising three books (and counting).

An avid reader and lifelong fan of the mystery and thriller genres, Ava loves to hear from you, so please feel free to visit www.avastrongauthor.com to learn more and stay in touch.

BOOKS BY AVA STRONG

REMI LAURENT FBI SUSPENSE THRILLER
THE DEATH CODE (Book #1)
THE MURDER CODE (Book #2)
THE MALICE CODE (Book #3)
THE VENGEANCE CODE (Book #4)
THE DECEPTION CODE (Book #5)
THE SEDUCTION CODE (Book #6)

ILSE BECK FBI SUSPENSE THRILLER
NOT LIKE US (Book #1)
NOT LIKE HE SEEMED (Book #2)
NOT LIKE YESTERDAY (Book #3)
NOT LIKE THIS (Book #4)
NOT LIKE SHE THOUGHT (Book #5)
NOT LIKE BEFORE (Book #6)
NOT LIKE NORMAL (Book #7)

STELLA FALL PSYCHOLOGICAL SUSPENSE THRILLER
HIS OTHER WIFE (Book #1)
HIS OTHER LIE (Book #2)
HIS OTHER SECRET (Book #3)
HIS OTHER MISTRESS (Book #4)
HIS OTHER LIFE (Book #5)
HIS OTHER TRUTH (Book #6)

DAKOTA STEELE FBI SUSPENSE THRILLER
WITHOUT MERCY (Book #1)
WITHOUT REMORSE (Book #2)
WITHOUT A PAST (Book #3)

www.ingramcontent.com/pod-product-compliance
Lightning Source LLC
Chambersburg PA
CBHW030617310726
48979CB00003B/764

* 9 7 8 1 0 9 4 3 9 4 9 2 3 *